'Our marriage is a tragedy.'

'No,' he denied. 'You merely insist on turning it into one.'

'Because I hate everything you stand for!'

'But you cannot make yourself hate the man,' he added, undisturbed by her denunciation.

Leona began to bac̲_____ _____ ft you, remember?'

'Then sent _____ _____ ls to make sure I _____ _____ vied.

'Letters to tell _____ _____ divorce!' she cried.

'The content of the letters came second to their true purpose.' He smiled. 'One every two weeks over the last two months. I found them most comforting.'

'Gosh, you are so conceited, it's a wonder you didn't marry yourself!'

'Such insults,' he sighed.

'I do not want to stay married to you.' She stated it bluntly.

'And I am not prepared to let you go.'

Michelle Reid grew up on the southern edges of Manchester, the youngest in a family of five lively children. But now she lives in the beautiful county of Cheshire with her busy executive husband and two grown-up daughters. She loves reading, the ballet, and playing tennis when she gets the chance. She hates cooking, cleaning, and despises ironing! Sleep she can do without, and produces some of her best written work during the early hours of the morning.

If you've enjoyed THE SHEIKH'S CHOSEN WIFE, you can revisit San Estéban, and enjoy the stories of Rafiq and Ethan. Look out for them in August and December 2002 paperback. Available where all Mills & Boon® books are sold.

Recent titles by the same author:

A SICILIAN SEDUCTION
THE UNFORGETTABLE HUSBAND
THE BELLINI BRIDE

THE SHEIKH'S CHOSEN WIFE

BY

MICHELLE REID

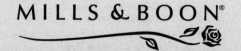

MILLS & BOON®

All the characters in this book have no existence outside the imagination of the author, and have no relation whatsoever to anyone bearing the same name or names. They are not even distantly inspired by any individual known or unknown to the author, and all the incidents are pure invention.

All Rights Reserved including the right of reproduction in whole or in part in any form. This edition is published by arrangement with Harlequin Enterprises II B.V. The text of this publication or any part thereof may not be reproduced or transmitted in any form or by any means, electronic or mechanical, including photocopying, recording, storage in an information retrieval system, or otherwise, without the written permission of the publisher.

This book is sold subject to the condition that it shall not, by way of trade or otherwise, be lent, resold, hired out or otherwise circulated without the prior consent of the publisher in any form of binding or cover other than that in which it is published and without a similar condition including this condition being imposed on the subsequent purchaser.

MILLS & BOON and MILLS & BOON with the Rose Device are registered trademarks of the publisher.

*First published in Great Britain 2002
Harlequin Mills & Boon Limited,
Eton House, 18-24 Paradise Road, Richmond, Surrey TW9 1SR*

© Michelle Reid 2002

ISBN 0 263 82920 0

*Set in Times Roman 10 on 11 pt.
01-0402-59954*

*Printed and bound in Spain
by Litografía Rosés, S.A., Barcelona*

CHAPTER ONE

DRESSED to go riding, in knee-length black leather boots, buff pants, a white shirt and a white *gutrah* held to his dark head by a plain black *agal*, Sheikh Hassan ben Khalifa Al-Qadim stepped into his private office and closed the door behind him. In his hand he held a newly delivered letter from England. On his desk lay three more. Walking across the room, he tossed the new letter onto the top of the other three then went to stand by the grilled window, fixing his eyes on a spot beyond the Al-Qadim Oasis, where reclaimed dry scrubland had been turned into miles of lush green fig groves.

Beyond the figs rose the sand-dunes. Majestic and proud, they claimed the horizon with a warning statement. Come any closer with your irrigation and expect retaliation, they said. One serious sandstorm, and years of hard labour could be turned back into arid wasteland.

A sigh eased itself from his body. Hassan knew all about the laws of the desert. He respected its power and its driving passion, its right to be master of its own destiny. And what he would really have liked to do at this very moment was to saddle up his horse, Zandor, then take off for those sand-dunes and allow them to dictate his future for him.

But he knew the idea was pure fantasy. For behind him lay four letters, all of which demanded he make those decisions for himself. And beyond the relative sanctuary of the four walls surrounding him lay a palace in waiting; his father, his half-brother, plus a thousand and one other people, all of whom believed they owned a piece of his so-called destiny.

So Zandor would have to stay in his stable. His beloved sand-dunes would have to wait a while to swallow him up. Making a half-turn, he stared grimly at the letters. Only one

had been opened: the first one, which he had tossed aside
with the contempt it had deserved. Since then he had left the
others sealed on his desk and had tried very hard to ignore
them.

But the time for burying his head in the sand was over.

A knock on the door diverted his attention. It would be
his most trusted aide, Faysal. Hassan recognised the lightness
of the knock. Sure enough the door opened and a short, fine-
boned man wearing the traditional white and pale blue robes
of their Arabian birthright appeared in its arched aperture,
where he paused and bowed his head, waiting to be invited
in or told to go.

'Come in, Faysal,' Hassan instructed a trifle impatiently.
Sometimes Faysal's rigid adherence to so-called protocol set
his teeth on edge.

With another deferential bow, Faysal moved to his master's bidding. Stepping into the room, he closed the door
behind him then used some rarely utilised initiative by walking across the room to come to a halt several feet from the
desk on the priceless carpet that covered, in part, the expanse
of polished blue marble between the desk and the door.

Hassan found himself staring at the carpet. His wife had
ordered it to be placed there, claiming the room's spartan
appearance invited no one to cross its austere threshold. The
fact that this was supposed to be the whole point had made
absolutely no difference to Leona. She had simply carried on
regardless, bringing many items into the room besides the
carpet. Such as the pictures now adorning the walls and the
beautiful ceramics and sculptures scattered around, all of
which had been produced by gifted artists native to the small
Gulf state of Rahman. Hassan had soon found he could no
longer lift his eyes without having them settle on an example
of local enterprise.

Yet it was towards the only western pieces Leona had
brought into the room that his eyes now drifted. The low
table and two overstuffed easy chairs had been placed by the
other window, where she would insist on making him sit with

her several times a day to enjoy the view while they drank tea and talked and touched occasionally as lovers do…

Dragging the *gutrah* from his head with almost angry fingers, Hassan tossed it aside then went to sit down in the chair behind his desk. 'Okay,' he said. 'What have you to tell me?'

'It is not good news, sir.' Faysal began with a warning. 'Sheikh Abdul is entertaining certain…factions at his summer palace. Our man on the inside confirms that the tone of their conversation warrants your most urgent attention.'

Hassan made no comment, but his expression hardened fractionally. 'And my wife?' he asked next.

'The Sheikha still resides in Spain, sir,' Faysal informed him, 'working with her father at the new resort of San Estéban, overseeing the furnishing of several villas about to be released for sale.'

Doing what she did best, Hassan thought grimly—and did not need to glance back at the two stuffed chairs to conjure up a vision of long silken hair the colour of a desert sunset, framing a porcelain smooth face with laughing green eyes and a smile that dared him to complain about her invasion of his private space. 'Trust me,' he could hear her say. 'It is my job to give great empty spaces a little soul and their own heartbeat.'

Well, the heartbeat had gone out of this room when she'd left it, and as for the soul…

Another sigh escaped him. 'How long do you think we have before they make their move?'

The slight tensing in Faysal's stance warned Hassan that he was not going to like what was coming. 'If you will forgive me for saying so, sir,' his aide apologised, 'with Mr Ethan Hayes also residing at her father's property, I would say that the matter has become most seriously urgent indeed.'

Since this was complete news to Hassan it took a moment for the full impact of this information to really sink in. Then he was suddenly on his feet and was swinging tensely away to glare at the sand-dunes again. Was she mad? he was thinking angrily. Did she have a death wish? Was she so indifferent to his feelings that she could behave like this?

Ethan Hayes. His teeth gritted together as an old familiar jealousy began mixing with his anger to form a much more volatile substance. He swung back to face Faysal. 'How long has Mr Hayes been in residence in San Estéban?'

Faysal made a nervous clearing of his throat. 'These seven days past,' he replied.

'And who else knows about this…? Sheikh Abdul?'

'It was discussed,' Faysal confirmed.

With a tight shifting of his long lean body, Hassan returned to his seat. 'Cancel all my appointments for the rest of the month,' he instructed, drawing his appointments diary towards him to begin scoring hard lines through the same busy pages. 'My yacht is berthed at Cadiz. Have it moved to San Estéban. Check that my plane is ready for an immediate take-off and ask Rafiq to come to me.'

The cold quality of the commands did nothing to dilute their grim purpose. 'If asked,' Faysal prompted, 'what reason do I give for your sudden decision to cancel your appointments?'

'I am about to indulge in a much needed holiday cruising the Mediterranean with my nice new toy,' Sheikh Hassan replied, and the bite in his tone made a complete mockery of the words spoken, for they both knew that the next few weeks promised to be no holiday. 'And Faysal…' Hassan stalled his aide as he was about to take his leave '…if anyone so much as whispers the word adultery in the same breath as my wife's name, they will not breathe again—you understand me?'

The other man went perfectly still, recognising the responsibility that was being laid squarely upon him. 'Yes, sir.' He bowed.

Hassan's grim nod was a dismissal. Left alone again, he leaned back in his chair and began frowning while he tried to decide how best to tackle this. His gaze fell on the small stack of letters. Reaching out with long fingers, he drew them

MICHELLE REID   9

towards him, picked out the only envelope with a broken seal and removed the single sheet of paper from inside. The content of the letter he ignored with the same dismissive contempt he had always applied to it. His interest lay only in the telephone number printed beneath the business logo. With an expression that said he resented having his hand forced like this, he took a brief glance at his watch, then was lifting up the telephone, fairly sure that his wife's lawyer would be in his London office at this time of the day.

The ensuing conversation was not a pleasant one, and the following conversation with his father-in-law even less so. He had just replaced the receiver and was frowning darkly over what Victor Frayne had said to him, when another knock sounded at the door. Hard eyes lanced towards it as the door swung open and Rafiq stepped into the room.

Though he was dressed in much the same clothes as Faysal was wearing, there the similarity between the two men ended. For where Faysal was short and thin and annoyingly effacing, Rafiq was a giant of a man who rarely kowtowed to anyone. Hassan warranted only a polite nod of the head, yet he knew Rafiq would willingly die for him if he was called upon to do so.

'Come in, shut the door, then tell me how you would feel about committing a minor piece of treason?' Hassan smoothly intoned.

Below the white *gutrah* a pair of dark eyes glinted. 'Sheikh Abdul?' Rafiq questioned hopefully.

'Unfortunately, no.' Hassan gave a half smile. 'I was in fact referring to my lovely wife, Leona...'

Dressed for the evening in a beaded slip-dress made of gold silk chiffon, Leona stepped into a pair of matching beaded mules then turned to look at herself in the mirror.

Her smooth russet hair had been caught up in a twist, and diamonds sparkled at her ears and throat. Overall, she supposed she looked okay, she decided, giving the thin straps at her shoulders a gentle tug so the dress settled comfortably over her slender frame. But the weight she had lost during the last year was most definitely showing, and she could have chosen a better colour to offset the unnatural paleness of her skin.

Too late to change, though, she thought with a dismissive shrug as she turned away from her reflection. Ethan was already waiting for her outside on the terrace. And, anyway, she wasn't out to impress anyone. She was merely playing stand-in for her father who had been delayed in London due to some urgent business with the family lawyer, which had left her and her father's business partner, Ethan, the only ones here to represent Hayes-Frayne at tonight's promotional dinner.

She grimaced as she caught up a matching black silk shawl and made for her bedroom door. In truth, she would rather not be going out at all tonight having only arrived back from San Estéban an hour ago. It had been a long day, and she had spent most of it melting in a Spanish heatwave because the air-conditioning system had not been working in the villa she had been attempting to make ready for viewing. So a long soak in a warm bath and an early night would have been her idea of heaven tonight, she thought wryly, as she went down the stairs to join Ethan.

He was half sitting on the terrace rail with a glass in his hand, watching the sun go down, but his head turned at her first step, and his mouth broke into an appreciative smile.

'Ravishing,' he murmured, sliding his lean frame upright.

'Thank you,' she replied. 'You don't look so bad yourself.'

His wry nod accepted the compliment and his grey eyes sparkled with lazy humour. Dressed in a black dinner suit and bow tie, he was a tall, dark, very attractive man with an easy smile and a famous eye for the ladies. Women adored him and he adored them but, thankfully, that mutual adoration had never raised its ugly head between the two of them.

Leona liked Ethan. She felt comfortable being with him. He was the Hayes in Hayes-Frayne, architects. Give

Ethan a blank piece of paper and he would create a fifty-storey skyscraper or a whole resort complete with sports clubs, shopping malls and, of course, holiday villas to die for, as with this new resort in San Estéban.

'Drink?' he suggested, already stepping towards the well stocked drinks trolley.

But Leona gave a shake of her head. 'Better not, if you want me to stay awake beyond ten o'clock,' she refused.

'That late? Next you'll be begging me to take you on to an all-night disco after the party.' He was mocking the fact that she was usually safely tucked up in bed by nine o'clock.

'Do you disco?' she asked him curiously.

'Not if I can help it,' he replied, discarding his own glass to come and take the shawl from her hand so he could drape it across her shoulders. 'The best I can offer in the name of dance is a soft shoe shuffle to something very slow, preferably in a darkened room, so that I don't damage my ego by revealing just how bad a shuffler I am.'

'You're such a liar.' Leona smiled. 'I've seen you dance a mean jive, once or twice.'

Ethan pulled a face at the reminder. 'Now you've really made me feel my age,' he complained. 'Next you'll be asking me what it was like to rock in the sixties.'

'You're not that old.' She was still smiling.

'Born in the mid-sixties,' he announced. 'To a free-loving mother who bopped with the best of them.'

'That makes you about the same age as Hass...'

And that was the point where everything died: the light banter, the laughter, the tail end of Hassan's name. Silence fell. Ethan's teasing grey eyes turned very sombre. He knew, of course, how painful this last year had been for her. No one mentioned Hassan's name in her presence, so to hear herself almost say it out loud caused tension to erupt between the both of them.

'It isn't too late to stop this craziness, you know,' Ethan murmured gently.

Her response was to drag in a deep breath and step right away from him. 'I don't want to stop it,' she quietly replied.

'Your heart does.'

'My heart is not making the decisions here.'

'Maybe you should let it.'

'Maybe you should mind your own business!'

Spinning on her slender heels Leona walked away from him to go and stand at the terrace rail, leaving Ethan behind wearing a rueful expression at the severity with which she had just slapped him down.

Out there at sea, the dying sun was throwing up slender fingers of fire into a spectacular vermilion sky. Down the hill below the villa, San Estéban was beginning to twinkle as it came into its own at the exit of the sun. And in between the town and the sun the ocean spread like satin with its brand-new purpose-built harbour already packed with smart sailing crafts of all shapes and sizes.

Up here on the hillside everything was so quiet and still even the cicadas had stopped calling. Leona wished that she could have some of that stillness, put her trembling emotions back where they belonged, under wraps, out of reach from pain and heartache.

Would these vulnerable feelings ever be that far out of reach? she then asked herself, and wasn't surprised to have a heavy sigh whisper from her. The beaded chiffon shawl slipped from her shoulders, prompting Ethan to come and gently lift it back in place again.

'Sorry,' he murmured. 'It wasn't my intention to upset you.'

I do it to myself, Leona thought bleakly. 'I just can't bear to talk about it,' she replied in what was a very rare glimpse at how badly she was hurting.

'Maybe you need to talk,' Ethan suggested.

But she just shook her head, as she consistently had done since she had arrived at her father's London house a year ago, looking emotionally shattered and announcing that her five-year marriage to Sheikh Hassan ben Khalifa Al-Qadim was over. Victor Frayne had tried every which way he could think of to find out what had happened. He'd even travelled out to Rahman to demand answers from Hassan, only to meet the same solid wall of silence he'd come up against with his daughter. The one thing Victor could say with any certainty was that Hassan was faring no better than Leona, though his dauntingly aloof son-in-law was more adept at hiding his emotions than Leona was. 'She sits here in London, he sits in Rahman. They don't talk to each other, never mind to anyone else! Yet you can feel the vibrations bouncing from one to the other across the thousands of miles separating them as if they are communicating by some unique telepathy that runs on pure pain! It's dreadful,' Victor had confided to Ethan. 'Something has to give some time.'

Eventually, it had done. Two months ago Leona had walked unannounced into the office of her family lawyer and had instructed him to begin divorce proceedings, on the grounds of irreconcilable differences. What had prompted her to pick that particular day in that particular month of a very long year no one understood, and Leona herself wasn't prepared to enlighten anyone. But there wasn't a person who knew her who didn't believe it was an action that had caused a trigger reaction, when a week later she had fallen foul of a virulent flu bug that had kept her housebound and bedridden for weeks afterwards.

But when she had recovered, at least she'd come back ready to face the world again. She had agreed to come here to San Estéban, for instance, and utilise her design skills on the completed villas.

She looked better for it too. Still too pale, maybe, but overall she'd begun to live a more normal day to day existence.

Ethan had no wish to send her back into hiding now she had come out of it, so he turned her to face him and pressed a light kiss to her brow. 'Come on,' he said briskly. 'Let's go and party!'

Finding her smile again, Leona nodded her agreement and

tried to appear as though she was looking forward to the evening. As they began to walk back across the terrace she felt a fine tingling at the back of her neck which instinctively warned her that someone was observing them.

The suspicion made her pause and turn to cast a frowning glance over their surroundings. She could see nothing untoward, but wasn't surprised by that. During the years she had lived in an Arab sheikhdom, married to a powerful and very wealthy man, she had grown used to being kept under constant, if very discreet, surveillance.

But that surveillance had been put in place for her own protection. This felt different—sinister. She even shivered.

'Something wrong?' Ethan questioned.

Leona shook her head and began walking again, but her frown stayed in place, because it wasn't the first time she'd experienced the sensation today. The same thing had happened as she'd left the resort site this afternoon, only she'd dismissed it then as her just being silly. She had always suspected that Hassan still kept an eye on her from a distance.

A car and driver had been hired for the evening, and both were waiting in the courtyard for them as they left the house. Having made sure she was comfortably settled, Ethan closed the side door and strode around the car to climb in beside her. As a man she had known for most of her adult life, Ethan was like a very fond cousin whose lean dark sophistication and reputed rakish life made her smile, rather than her heart flutter as other women would do in his company.

He'd never married. 'Never wanted to,' he'd told her once. 'Marriage diverts your energy away from your ambition, and I haven't met the woman for whom I'm prepared to let that happen.'

When she'd told Hassan what Ethan had said, she'd expected him to say something teasing like, May Allah help him when he does, for I know the feeling! But instead he'd looked quite sombre and had said nothing at all. At the time, she'd thought he'd been like that because he'd still been harbouring jealous suspicions about Ethan's feelings for her.

It had been a long time before she'd come to understand that the look had had nothing at all to do with Ethan.

'The Petronades yacht looks pretty impressive.' Ethan's smooth deep voice broke into her thoughts. 'I watched it sail into the harbour tonight while I was waiting for you on the terrace.'

Leandros Petronades was the main investor in San Estéban. He was hosting the party tonight for very exclusive guests whom he had seduced into taking a tour of the new resort, with an invitation to arrive in style on his yacht and enjoy its many luxurious facilities.

'At a guess, I would say it has to be the biggest in the harbour, considering its capacity to sleep so many people,' Leona smiled.

'Actually no, it wasn't,' Ethan replied with a frown. 'There's another yacht tied up that has to be twice the size.'

'The commercial kind?' Leona suggested, aware that the resort was fast becoming the fashionable place to visit.

'Not big enough.' Ethan shook his head. 'It's more likely to belong to one of Petronades' rich cronies. Another heavy investor in the resort, maybe.'

There were enough of them, Leona acknowledged. From being a sleepy little fishing port a few years ago, with the help of some really heavyweight investors San Estéban had grown into a large, custom-built holiday resort, which now sprawled in low-rise, Moorish elegance over the hills surrounding the bay.

So why Hassan's name slid back into her head Leona had no idea. Because Hassan didn't even own a yacht, nor had he ever invested in any of her father's projects, as far as she knew.

Irritated with herself, she turned her attention to what was happening outside the car. On the beach waterfront people strolled, enjoying the light breeze coming off the water.

It was a long time since she could remember strolling anywhere herself with such freedom. Marrying an Arab had brought with it certain restrictions on her freedom, which were not all due to the necessity of conforming to expectations regarding women. Hassan occupied the august position of being the eldest son and heir to the small but oil-rich Gulf state of Rahman. As his wife, Leona had become a member of Rahman's exclusive hierarchy, which in turn made everything she said or did someone else's property. So she'd learned very quickly to temper her words, to think twice before she went anywhere, especially alone. Strolling just for the sake of just doing it would have been picked upon and dissected for no other reason than interest's sake, so she had learned not to do it.

This last year she hadn't gone out much because to be seen out had drawn too much speculation as to why she was in London and alone. In Rahman she was known as Sheikh Hassan's pretty English Sheikha. In London she was known as the woman who gave up every freedom to marry her Arabian prince.

A curiosity in other words. Curiosities were blatantly stared at, and she didn't want to offend Arab sensibilities by having her failed marriage speculated upon in the British press, so she'd lived a quiet life.

It was a thought that made Leona smile now, because her life in Rahman had been far less quiet than it had become once she'd returned to London.

The car had almost reached the end of the street where the new harbour was situated. There were several large yachts moored up—and Leandros Petronades' elegant white-hulled boat was easy to recognise because it was lit up like a showboat for the party. Yet it was the yacht moored next to it that caught her attention. It was huge, as Ethan had said—twice the length and twice the height of its neighbour. It was also shrouded in complete darkness. With its dark-painted hull, it looked as if it was crouching there like a large sleek cat, waiting to leap on its next victim.

The car turned and began driving along the top of the harbour wall taking them towards a pair of wrought iron gates, which cordoned off the area where the two yachts were tied.

Climbing out of the car, Leona stood looking round while she waited for Ethan to join her. It was even darker here than she had expected it to be, and she felt a distinct chill shiver down her spine when she realised they were going to have to pass the unlit boat to reach the other.

Ethan's hand found her arm. As they walked towards the gates, their car was already turning round to go back the way it had come. The guard manning the gates merely nodded his dark head and let them by without a murmur, then disappeared into the shadows.

'Conscientious chap,' Ethan said dryly.

Leona didn't answer. She was too busy having to fight a sudden attack of nerves that set butterflies fluttering inside her stomach. Okay, she tried to reason, so she hadn't put herself in the social arena much recently, therefore it was natural that she should suffer an attack of nerves tonight.

Yet some other part of her brain was trying to insist that her attack of nerves had nothing to do with the party. It was so dark and so quiet here that even their footsteps seemed to echo with a sinister ring.

Sinister? Picking up on the word, she questioned it impatiently. What was the matter with her? Why was everything sinister all of a sudden? It was a hot night—a beautiful night—she was twenty-nine years old, and about to do what most twenty-nine-year-olds did: party when they got the chance!

'Quite something, hmm?' Ethan remarked as they walked into the shadow of the larger yacht.

But Leona didn't want to look. Despite the tough talking-to she had just given herself, the yacht bothered her. The whole situation was beginning to worry her. She could feel her heart pumping unevenly against her breast, and just about every nerve-end she possessed was suddenly on full alert for no other reason than—

It was then that she heard it—nothing more than a whispering sound in the shadows, but it was enough to make her go perfectly still. So did Ethan. Almost at the same moment the darkness itself seemed to take on a life of its own by shifting and swaying before her eyes.

The tingling sensation on the back of her neck returned with a vengeance. 'Ethan,' she said jerkily. 'I don't think I like this.'

'No,' he answered tersely. 'Neither do I.'

That was the moment when they saw them, first one dark shape, then another, and another, emerging from the shadows until they turned themselves into Arabs wearing dark robes, with darkly sober expressions.

'Oh, dear God,' she breathed. 'What's happening?'

But she already knew the answer. It was a fear she'd had to live with from the day she'd married Hassan. She was British. She had married an Arab who was a very powerful man. The dual publicity her disappearance could generate was in itself worth its weight in gold to political fanatics wanting to make a point.

Something she should have remembered earlier, then the word 'sinister' would have made a lot more sense, she realised, as Ethan's arm pressed her hard up against him.

Further down the harbour wall the lights from the Petronades boat were swinging gently. Here, beneath the shadow of the other, the ring of men was steadily closing in. Her heart began to pound like a hammer drill. Ethan couldn't hold her any closer if he tried, and she could almost taste his tension. He, too, knew exactly what was going to happen.

'Keep calm,' he gritted down at her. 'When I give the word, lose your shoes and run.'

He was going to make a lunge for them and try to break the ring so she could have a small chance to escape. 'No,' she protested, and clutched tightly at his jacket sleeve. 'Don't do it. They might hurt you if you do!'

'Just go, Leona!' he ground back at her, then, with no more warning than that, he was pulling away, and almost in the same movement he threw himself at the two men closest to him.

It was then that all hell broke loose. While Leona stood there frozen in horror watching all three men topple to the ground in a huddle, the rest of the ring leapt into action. Fear for her life sent a surge of adrenaline rushing through her blood. Dry-mouthed, stark-eyed, she was just about to do as Ethan had told her and run, when she heard a hard voice rasp out a command in Arabic. In a state of raw panic she swung round in its direction, expecting someone to be almost upon her, only to find to her confusion that the ring of men had completely bypassed her, leaving her standing here alone with only one other man.

It was at that point that she truly stopped functioning—heart, lungs, her ability to hear what was happening to Ethan—all connections to her brain simply closed down to leave only her eyes in full, wretched focus.

Tall and dark, whip-cord lean, he possessed an aura about him that warned of great physical power lurking beneath the dark robes he was wearing. His skin was the colour of sun-ripened olives, his eyes as black as a midnight sky, and his mouth she saw was thin, straight and utterly unsmiling.

'Hassan.' She breathed his name into the darkness.

The curt bow he offered her came directly from an excess of noble arrogance built into his ancient genes. 'As you see,' Sheikh Hassan smoothly confirmed.

CHAPTER TWO

A BUBBLE of hysteria ballooned in her throat. 'But—why?' she choked in strangled confusion.

Hassan was not given the opportunity to answer before another fracas broke out somewhere behind her. Ethan ground her name out. It was followed by some thuds and scuffles. As she turned on a protesting gasp to go to him, someone else spoke with a grating urgency and Hassan caught her wrist, long brown fingers closing round fleshless skin and bone, to hold her firmly in place.

'Call them off!' she cried out shrilly.

'Be silent,' he returned in a voice like ice.

It shocked her, really shocked her, because never in their years together had he ever used that tone on her. Turning her head, she stared at him in pained astonishment, but Hassan wasn't even looking at her. His attention was fixed on a spot near the gates. With a snap of his fingers his men began scattering like bats on the wing, taking a frighteningly silent Ethan with them.

'Where are they going with him?' Leona demanded anxiously.

Hassan didn't answer. Another man came to stand directly behind her and, glancing up, she found herself gazing into yet another familiar face.

'Rafiq,' she murmured, but that was all she managed to say before Hassan was reclaiming her attention by snaking an arm around her waist and pulling her towards him. Her breasts made contact with solid muscle; her thighs suddenly burned like fire as they felt the unyielding power in his. Her eyes leapt up to clash with his eyes. It was like tumbling into oblivion. He looked so very angry, yet so very—

'Shh,' he cautioned. 'It is absolutely imperative that you do exactly as I say. For there is a car coming down the causeway and we cannot afford to have any witnesses.'

'Witnesses to what?' she asked in bewilderment.

There was a pause, a smile that was not quite a smile because it was too cold, too calculating, too—

'Your abduction,' he smoothly informed her.

Standing there in his arms, feeling trapped by a word that sounded totally alien falling from those lips she'd thought she knew so well, Leona released a constricted gasp then was totally silenced.

Car headlights suddenly swung in their direction. Rafiq moved and the next thing that she knew a shroud of black muslin was being thrown over her head. For a split second she couldn't believe what was actually happening! Then Hassan released his grasp so the muslin could unfurl right down to her ankles: she was being shrouded in an *abaya*.

Never had she *ever* been forced to wear such a garment! 'Oh, how could you?' she wrenched out, already trying to drag the *abaya* off again.

Strong arms firmly subdued her efforts. 'Now, you have two choices here, my darling.' Hassan's grim voice sounded close to her ear. 'You can either come quietly, of your own volition, or Rafiq and I will ensure that you do so—understand?'

Understand? Oh, yes, Leona thought painfully, she understood fully that she was being recovered like a lost piece of property! 'I'll never forgive you for this,' she breathed thickly.

His response was to wedge her between himself and Rafiq and then begin hustling her quickly forward. Feeling hot, trapped and blinded by the *abaya*, she had no idea where they were taking her.

Her frightened gasp brought Hassan's hand to cup her elbow. 'Be calm,' he said quietly. 'I am here.'

His reassurance was no assurance to Leona as he began urging her to walk ahead of him. The ground beneath her feet gave way to something much less substantial. Through the thin soles of her shoes she could feel a ridged metal surface, and received a cold sense of some dark space yawning beneath it.

'What is this?' she questioned shakily.

'The gangway to my yacht,' Hassan replied.

His yacht, she repeated, and thought of the huge dark vessel squatting in the darkness. 'New toy, Hassan?' she hit out deridingly.

'I knew you would be enchanted,' he returned. 'Watch your step!' he cautioned sharply when the open toe of her flimsy shoe caught on one of the metal ridges.

But she couldn't watch her step because the wretched *abaya* was in the way! So she tripped, tried to right herself, felt the slender heel of her shoe twist out from beneath her. Instinct made her put out a hand in a bid to save herself. But once again the *abaya* was in the way and, as she tried to grapple with it, the long loose veil of muslin tangled around her ankles and she lurched drunkenly forward. The sheer impetus of the lurch lost Hassan his guiding grip on her arm. As the sound of her own stifled cry mingled with the roughness of his, Leona knew she hadn't a hope of saving herself. In the few split seconds it all took to happen, she had a horrible vision of deep dark water between the boat and the harbour wall waiting to suck her down, with the wretched *abaya* acting as her burial shroud.

Then hard hands were gripping her waist and roughly righting her; next she was being scooped up and crushed hard against a familiar chest. She curled into that chest like a vulnerable child and began shaking all over while she listened to Hassan cursing and swearing beneath his breath as he carried her, and Rafiq answering with soothing tones from somewhere ahead.

Onto the yacht, across the deck, Leona could hear doors being flung wide as they approached. By the time Hassan decided that it was safe to set her down on her own feet again, reaction was beginning to set in.

Shock and fright changed to a blistering fury the moment her feet hit the floor. Breaking free, she spun away from him, then began dragging the *abaya* off over her head with angry, shaking fingers. Light replaced darkness, sweet cool air replaced suffocating heat. Tossing the garment to the floor, she swung round to face her two abductors with her green eyes flashing and the rest of her shimmering with an incandescent rage.

Both Hassan and Rafiq stood framed by a glossy wood doorway, studying her with differing expressions. Both wore long black tunics beneath dark blue cloaks cinched in at the waist with wide black sashes. Dark blue *gutrahs* framed their lean dark faces. One neatly bearded, the other clean-shaven and sleek. Both held themselves with an indolent arrogance that was a challenge as they waited to receive her first furious volley.

Her heart flipped over and tumbled to her stomach, her feeling of an impossible-to-fight admiration for these two people, only helping to infuriate her all the more. For who were they—*what* were they—that they believed they had the right to treat her like this?

She began to walk towards them. Her hair had escaped from its twist and was now tumbling like fire over her shoulders, and somewhere along the way she had lost her shawl and shoes. Without the help of her shoes, the two men towered over her, indomitable and proud, dark brown eyes offering no hint of apology.

Her gaze fixed itself somewhere between them, her hands closed into two tightly clenched fists at her side. The air actually stung with an electric charge of anticipation. 'I demand to see Ethan,' she stated very coldly.

It was clearly the last thing either was expecting her to say. Rafiq stiffened infinitesimally, Hassan looked as if she could not have insulted him more if she'd tried.

His eyes narrowed, his mouth grew thin, his handsome sleek features hardened into polished rock. Beneath the dark robes, Leona saw his wide chest expand and remain that way as, with a sharp flick of a hand, he sent Rafiq sweeping out of the room.

As the door closed them in, the sudden silence stifled almost as much as the *abaya* had done. Neither moved, neither spoke for the space of thirty long heart-throbbing seconds, while Hassan stared coldly down at her and she stared at some obscure point near his right shoulder.

Years of loving this one man, she was thinking painfully. Five years of living the dream in a marriage she had believed was so solid that nothing could ever tear it apart. Now she couldn't even bring herself to focus on his face properly in case the feelings she now kept deeply suppressed inside her came surging to the surface and spilled out on a wave of broken-hearted misery. For their marriage was over. They both knew it was over. He should not have done this to her. It hurt so badly that he could treat her this way that she didn't think she was ever going to forgive him for it.

Hassan broke the silence by releasing the breath he had been holding onto. 'In the interests of harmony, I suggest you restrain from mentioning Ethan Hayes in my presence,' he advised, then simply stepped right past her to walk across the room to a polished wood counter which ran the full length of one wall.

As she followed the long, lean, subtle movement of his body through desperately loving eyes, fresh fury leapt up to save her again. 'But who else would I ask about when I've just watched your men beat him up and drag him away?' she threw after him.

'They did not beat him up.' Flicking open a cupboard door, he revealed a fridge stocked with every conceivable form of liquid refreshment.

'They fell on him like a flock of hooligans!'

'They subdued his enthusiasm for a fight.'

'He was defending me!'

'That is my prerogative.'

Her choked laugh at that announcement dropped scorn all

over it. 'Sometimes your arrogance stuns even me!' she informed him scathingly.

The fridge door shut with a thud. 'And your foolish refusal to accept wise advice when it is offered to you stuns me!'

Twisting round, Hassan was suddenly revealing an anger that easily matched her own. His eyes were black, his expression harsh, his mouth snapped into a grim line. In his hand he held a bottle of mineral water which he slammed down on the cabinet top, then he began striding towards her, big and hard and threatening.

'I don't know what's the matter with you,' she burst out bewilderedly. 'Why am I under attack when I haven't done anything?'

'You dare to ask that, when this is the first time we have looked upon each other in a year—yet all you can think about is Ethan Hayes?'

'Ethan isn't your enemy,' she persisted stubbornly.

'No.' Thinly said. Then something happened within his eyes that set her heart shuddering. He came to a stop a bare foot away from her. 'But he is most definitely yours,' he said.

She didn't want him this close and took a step back. 'I don't know what you mean,' she denied.

He closed the gap again. 'A married woman openly living with a man who is not her husband carries a heavy penalty in Rahman.'

'Are you daring to suggest that Ethan and I *sleep* together?' Her eyes went wide with utter affront.

'Do you?'

The question was like a slap to the face. 'No we do not!'

'Prove it,' he challenged.

Surprise had her falling back another step. 'But you know Ethan and I don't have that kind of relationship,' she insisted.

'And, I repeat,' he said, 'prove it.'

Nerve-ends began to fray when she realised he was being serious. 'I can't,' she admitted, then went quite pale when she felt forced to add, 'But you know I wouldn't sleep with him, Hassan. You *know* it,' she emphasised with a painfully thickening tone which placed a different kind of darkness in his eyes.

It came from understanding and pity. And she hated him for that also! Hated and loved and hurt with a power that was worse than any other torture he could inflict.

'Then explain to me, please,' he persisted nonetheless, 'when you openly live beneath the same roof as he does, how I convince my people of this certainty you believe I have in your fidelity?'

'But Ethan and I haven't spent one night alone together in the villa,' she protested. 'My father has always been there with us until he was delayed in London today!'

'Quite.' Hassan nodded. 'Now you understand why you have been snatched from the brink of committing the ultimate sin in the eyes of our people. There,' he said with a dismissive flick of the hand. 'I am your saviour, as is my prerogative.'

With that, and having neatly tied the whole thing off to his own satisfaction, he turned and walked away— Leaving Leona to flounder in his smooth, slick logic and with no ready argument to offer.

'I don't believe you are real sometimes,' she sent shakily after him. 'Did it never occur to you that I didn't want *snatching from the brink*?'

Sarcasm abounding, Hassan merely pulled the *gutrah* from his head and tossed it aside, then returned to the bottle of water. 'It was time,' he said, swinging the fridge door open again. 'You have had long enough to sulk.'

'I wasn't sulking!'

'Whatever,' he dismissed with a shrug, then chose a bottle of white wine and closed the door. 'It was time to bring the impasse to an end.'

Impasse, Leona repeated. He believed their failed marriage was merely stuck in an *impasse*. 'I'm not coming back to you,' she declared, then turned away to pretend to take an interest in her surroundings, knowing that his grim silence was denying her the right to choose.

They were enclosed in what she could only presume was a private stateroom furnished in subtle shades of cream faced with richly polished rosewood. It was all so beautifully designed that it was almost impossible to see the many doors built into the walls except for the wood-framed doors they had entered through. And it was the huge deep-sprung divan taking pride of place against a silk-lined wall, that told her exactly what the room's function was.

Although the bed was not what truly captured her attention, but the pair of big easy chairs standing in front of a low table by a set of closed cream velvet curtains. As her heart gave a painful twist in recognition, she sent a hand drifting up to her eyes. Oh, Hassan, she thought despairingly, don't do this to me…

She had seen the chairs, Hassan noted, studying the way she was standing there looking like an exquisitely fragile, perfectly tooled art-deco sculpture in her slender gown of gold. And he didn't know whether to tell her so or simply weep at how utterly bereft she looked.

In the end he chose a third option and took a rare sip at the white wine spritzer he had just prepared for her. The forbidden alcohol content in the drink might be diluted but he felt it hit his stomach and almost instantly enter his bloodstream with an injection of much appreciated fire.

'You've lost weight,' he announced, and watched her chin come up, watched her wonderful hair slide down her slender back and her hand drop slowly to her side while she took a steadying breath before she could bring herself to turn and face him.

'I've been ill—with the flu,' she answered flatly.

'That was weeks ago,' he dismissed, uncaring that he was revealing to her just how close an eye he had been keeping on her from a distance. The fact that she showed no surprise told him that she had guessed as much anyway. 'After a virus such as influenza the weight recovery is usually swift.'

'And you would know, of course,' she drawled, mocking the fact that he had not suffered a day's illness in his entire life.

'I know *you*,' he countered, 'and your propensity for slipping into a decline when you are unhappy...'

'I was *ill*, not unhappy.'

'You missed me. I missed you. Why try to deny it?'

'May I have one of those?' Indicating towards the drink he held in his hand was her way of telling him she was going to ignore those kind of comments.

'It is yours,' he explained, and offered the glass out to her.

She looked at the glass, long dusky lashes flickering over her beautiful green eyes when she realised he was going to make her come and get the drink. Would she do it? he wondered curiously. Would she allow herself to come this close, when they both knew she would much rather turn and run?

But his beautiful wife had never been a coward. No matter how she might be feeling inside, he had never known her to run from a challenge. Even when she had left him last year she had done so with courage, not cowardice. And she did not let him down now as her silk stockinged feet began to tread the cream carpet until she was in reach of the glass.

'Thank you.' The wine spritzer was taken from him and lifted to her mouth. She sipped without knowing she had been offered the glass so she would place her lips where his lips had been.

Her pale throat moved as she swallowed; her lips came away from the glass wearing a seductively alluring wine glossed bloom. He watched her smother a sigh, watched her look anywhere but directly at him, was aware that she had not looked him in the face since removing the *abaya*, just as she had stopped looking at him weeks before she left Rahman. And he had to suppress his own sigh as he felt muscles tighten all over his body in his desire to reach out, draw her close and make her look at him!

But this was not the time to play the demanding husband. She would reject him as she had rejected him many times a year ago. What hurt him the most about remembering those bleak interludes was not his own angry frustration but the grim knowledge that it had been herself she had been denying.

'Was the Petronades yacht party an elaborate set-up?' she asked suddenly.

A brief smile stretched his mouth, and it was a very self-mocking smile because he had truly believed she was as concentrated on his close physical presence as he was on hers. But, no. As always, Leona's mind worked in ways that continually managed to surprise him.

'The party was genuine.' He answered the question. 'Your father's sudden inability to get here in time to attend it was not.'

At least his honesty almost earned him a direct glance of frowning puzzlement before she managed to divert it to his right ear. 'But you've just finished telling me that I was snatched because my father was—'

'I know,' he cut in, not needing to hear her explain what he already knew—which was that this whole thing had been very carefully set up and co-ordinated with her father's assistance. 'There are many reasons why you are standing here with me right now, my darling,' he murmured gently. 'Most of which can wait for another time to go into.'

The *my darling* sent her back a defensive step. The realisation that her own father had plotted against her darkened her lovely eyes. 'Tell me now,' she insisted.

But Hassan just shook his head. 'Now is for me,' he informed her softly. 'Now is my moment to bask in the fact that you are back where you belong.'

It was really a bit of bad timing that her feet should use that particular moment to tread on the discarded *abaya*, he supposed, watching as she looked down, saw, then grew angry all over again.

'By abduction?' Her chin came up, contempt shimmering along her finely shaped bones. 'By plots and counter-plots and by removing a woman's right to decide for herself?'

He grimaced at her very accurate description. 'We are by nature a romantic people,' he defended. 'We love drama and poetry and tragic tales of star-crossed lovers who lose each other and travel the caverns of hell in their quest to find their way back together again.'

He saw the tears. He had said too much. Reaching out, he caught the glass just before it slipped from her nerveless fingers. 'Our marriage is a tragedy,' she told him thickly.

'No,' he denied, putting the hapless glass aside. 'You merely insist on turning it into one.'

'Because I hate everything you stand for!'

'But you cannot make yourself hate the man,' he added, undisturbed by her denunciation.

Leona began to back away because there was something seriously threatening about the sudden glow she caught in his eyes. 'I left you, remember?'

'Then sent me letters at regular intervals to make sure I remembered you,' he drawled.

'Letters to tell you I want a divorce!' she cried.

'The content of the letters came second to their true purpose.' He smiled. 'One every two weeks over the last two months. I found them most comforting.'

'Gosh, you are so conceited it's a wonder you didn't marry yourself!'

'Such insults.' He sighed.

'Will you stop stalking me as if I am a hunted animal?' she cried.

'Stop backing away like one.'

'I do not want to stay married to you.' She stated it bluntly.

'And I am not prepared to let you go. There,' he said. 'We have reached another impasse. Which one of us is going to win the higher ground this time, do you think?'

Looking at him standing there, arrogant and proud yet so much her kind of man that he made her legs go weak, Leona knew exactly which one of them possessed the higher ground. Which was also why she had to keep him at arm's length at all costs. He could fell her in seconds, because he was right; she didn't hate him, she adored him. And that scared her so much that when his hand came up, long fingertips brushing gently across her trembling mouth, she almost fainted on the sensation that shot from her lips to toe tips.

She pulled right away. His eyebrow arched. It mocked and challenged as he responded by curling the hand around her nape.

'Stop it,' she said, and lifted up her hand to use it as a brace against his chest.

Beneath dark blue cotton she discovered a silk-smooth, hard-packed body pulsing with heat and an all-too-familiar masculine potency. Her mouth went dry; she tried to breathe and found that she couldn't. Helplessly she lifted her eyes up to meet with his.

'Seeing me now, hmm?' he softly taunted. 'Seeing this man with these eyes you like to drown in, and this nose you like to call dreadful but usually have trouble from stopping your fingers from stroking? And let us not forget this mouth you so like to feel crushed hotly against your own delightful mouth.'

'Don't you dare!' she protested, seeing what was coming and already beginning to shake all over at the terrifying prospect of him finding out what a weak-willed coward she was.

'Why not?' he countered, offering her one of his lazily sensual, knowing smiles that said he knew better than she did what she really wanted—and he began to lower his dark head.

'Tell me first.' Sheer desperation made her fly into impulsive speech. 'If I am here on this beautiful yacht that belongs to you—is there another yacht just like it out there somewhere where your second wife awaits her turn?'

In the sudden suffocating silence that fell between them Leona found herself holding her breath as she watched his face pale to a frightening stillness. For this was provocation of the worst kind to an Arab and her heart began pounding madly because she just didn't know how he was going to respond. Hassan possessed a shocking temper, though he had never unleashed it on her. But now, as she stood here with her fingers still pressed against his breastbone, she could feel the danger in him—could almost taste her own fear as she waited to see how he was going to respond.

What he did was to take a step back from her. Cold, aloof, he changed into the untouchable prince in the single blink of an ebony eyelash. 'Are you daring to imply that I could be guilty of treating my wives unequally?' he responded.

In the interim wave of silence that followed, Leona stared at him through eyes that had stopped seeing anything as his reply rocked the very axis she stood upon. She knew she had prompted it but she still had not expected it, and now she found she couldn't breathe, couldn't even move as fine cracks began to appear in her defences.

'You actually went and did it, and married again,' she whispered, then completely shattered. Emotionally, physically, she felt herself fragment into a thousand broken pieces beneath his stone-cold, cruel gaze.

Hassan didn't see it coming. He should have done, he knew that, but he had been too angry to see anything but his own affronted pride. So when she turned and ran he didn't expect it. By the time he had pulled his wits together enough to go after her Leona was already flying through the door on a flood of tears.

The tears blinded what was ahead of her, the *abaya* having prevented her from taking stock of her surroundings as they'd arrived. Hassan heard Rafiq call out a warning, reached the door as Leona's cry curdled the very air surrounding them and she began to fall.

What he had managed to prevent by the skin of his teeth only a half-hour before now replayed itself before his helpless eyes. Only it was not the dark waters of the Mediterranean she fell into but the sea of cream carpet that ran from room to room and down a wide flight of three shallow stairs that led down into the yacht's main foyer.

CHAPTER THREE

CURSING and swearing in seething silence, Hassan prowled three sides of the bed like a caged tiger while the yacht's Spanish medic checked her over.

'No bones broken, as far as I can tell,' the man said. 'No obvious blow to the head.'

'Then why is she unconscious?' he growled out furiously.

'Shock—winded,' the medic suggested, gently laying aside a frighteningly limp hand. 'It has only been a few minutes, sir.'

But a few minutes was a lifetime when you felt so guilty you wished it was yourself lying there, Hassan thought harshly.

'A cool compress would be a help—'

A cool compress. 'Rafiq.' The click of his fingers meant the job would be done.

The sharp sound made Leona flinch. On a single, lithe leap Hassan was suddenly stretched out across the bed and leaning over her. The medic drew back; Rafiq paused in his step.

'Open your eyes.' Hassan turned her face towards him with a decidedly unsteady hand.

Her eyes fluttered open to stare up at him blankly. 'What happened?' she mumbled.

'You fell down some stairs,' he gritted. 'Now tell me where you hurt.'

A frown began to pucker her smooth brow as she tried to remember.

'Concentrate,' he rasped, diverting her mind away from what had happened. 'Do you hurt anywhere?'

She closed her eyes again, and he watched her make a mental inventory of herself then give a small shake of her head. 'I think I'm okay.' She opened her eyes again, looked directly into his, saw his concern, his anguish, the burning fires of guilt—and then she remembered *why* she'd fallen.

Aching tears welled up again. From coldly plunging his imaginary knife into her breast, he now felt it enter his own. 'You really went and did it,' she whispered.

'No, I did not,' he denied. 'Get out,' he told their two witnesses.

The room emptied like water down a drain, leaving them alone again, confronting each other again. It was dangerous. He wanted to kiss her so badly he could hardly breathe. She was his. He was hers! They should not be in this warring situation!

'No—remain still!' he commanded when she attempted to move. 'Don't even breathe unless you have to do so! Why are females so *stupid*?' he bit out like a curse. 'You insult me with your suspicions. You goad me into a response, and when it is not the one you want to hear you slay me with your pain!'

'I didn't mean to fall down the stairs,' she pointed out.

'I wasn't talking about the fall!' he bit out, then glared down into her confused, hurt, vulnerable eyes for a split second longer. 'Oh, Allah give me strength,' he gritted, and gave in to himself and took her trembling mouth by storm.

If he had kissed her in any other way Leona would have fought him with her very last breath. But she liked the storm; she *needed* the storm so she could allow herself to be swept away. Plus he was trembling, and she liked that too. Liked to know that she still had the power to reduce the prince in him to this vulnerable mass of smashed emotion.

And she'd missed him. She'd missed feeling his length lying alongside her length, had missed the weight of his thighs pressing down on her own. She'd missed his kiss, hungry, urgent, insistent…wanting. Like a banquet after a year of long, hard fasting, she fed greedily on every deep, dark, sensual delight. Lips, teeth, tongue, taste. She reached for his chest, felt the strong beat of his heart as she glided her palms beneath the fabric of his top robe where only the thin cotton of his tunic came between them and tightly muscled, satin-smooth flesh. When she reached his shoulders her fingers curled themselves into tightly padded muscle then stayed there, inviting him to take what he liked.

He took her breasts, stroking and shaping before moving on to follow the slender curve of her body. Long fingers claimed her hips, then drew her against the force of his. Fire bloomed in her belly, for this was her man, the love of her life. She would never, ever, find herself another. What he touched belonged to him. What he desired he could have.

What he did was bring a cruelly abrupt end to it by rising in a single fluid movement to land on his feet beside the bed, leaving her to flounder on the hard rocks of rejection while he stood there with his back to her, fighting a savage battle with himself.

'Why?' she breathed in thick confusion.

'We are not animals,' he ground back. 'We have issues to deal with that must preclude the hungry coupling at which we already know we both excel.'

It served as a dash of water in her face; and he certainly possessed good aim, Leona noted as she came back to reality with a shivering gasp. 'What issues?' she challenged cynically. 'The issue of what we have left besides the excellent sex?'

He didn't answer. Instead he made one of her eyebrows arch as he snatched up her spritzer and grimly downed the lot. There was a man at war with himself as well as with her, Leona realised, knowing Hassan hardly ever touched alcohol, and only then when he was under real stress.

Sitting up, she was aware of a few aches and bruises as she gingerly slid her feet to the floor. 'I want to go home,' she announced.

'This is home,' he replied. 'For the next few weeks, anyway.'

Few weeks? Coming just as gingerly to her feet, Leona stared at his rigid back—which was just another sign that

Hassan was not functioning to his usual standards, because no Arab worthy of the race would deliberately set his back to anyone. It was an insult of the worst kind.

Though she had seen his back a lot during those few months before she'd eventually left him, Leona recalled with a familiar sinking feeling inside. Not because he had wished to insult her, she acknowledged, but because he had refused to face what they had both known was happening to their marriage. In the end, she had taken the initiative away from him.

'Where are my shoes?'

The surprisingly neutral question managed to bring him swinging round to glance at her feet. 'Rafiq has them.'

Dear Rafiq, Leona thought wryly, Hassan's ever-loyal partner in crime. Rafiq was an Al-Qadim. A man who had attended the same schools, the same universities, the same everything as Hassan had done. Equals in many ways, prince and lowly servant in others. It was a complicated relationship that wound around the status of birth and the ranks of power.

'Perhaps you would be kind enough to ask him to give them back to me.' Even she knew you didn't *command* Rafiq to do anything. He was a law unto himself—and Hassan. Rafiq was a maverick. A man of the desert, yet not born of the desert; fiercely proud, fiercely protective of his right to be master of his own decisions.

'For what purpose?'

Leona's chin came up, recognising the challenge in his tone. She offered him a cool, clear look. 'I am not staying here, Hassan,' she told him flatly. 'Even if I have to book into a hotel in San Estéban to protect your dignity, I am leaving this boat now, tonight.'

His expression grew curious, a slight smile touched his mouth. 'Strong swimmer, are you?' he questioned lazily.

It took a few moments for his taunt to truly sink in, then she was moving, darting across the room and winding her way between the two strategically placed chairs and the accompanying table to reach for the curtains. Beyond the glass, all she could see was inky darkness. Maybe she was on the seaward side of the boat, she told herself in an effort to calm the sudden sting of alarm that slid down her spine.

Hassan quickly disabused her of that frail hope. 'We left San Estéban minutes after we boarded.'

It was only then that she felt it: just the softest hint of a vibration beneath the soles of her feet that told of smooth and silently running engines. This truly was an abduction, she finally accepted, and turned slowly back round to face him.

'Why?' she breathed.

It was like a replay of what had already gone before, only this time it was serious—more serious than Leona had even begun to imagine. For she knew this man—knew he was not given to flights of impulse just for the hell of it. Everything he did had to have a reason, and was always preceded by meticulous planning which took time he would not waste, and effort he would not move unless he felt he absolutely had to do.

Hassan's small sigh conveyed that he too knew that this was where the prevarication ended. 'There are problems at home,' he informed her soberly. 'My father's health is failing.'

His father... Anger swiftly converted itself into anxious concern for her father-in-law. Sheikh Khalifa had been frail in health for as long as she had known him. Hassan doted on him and devoted most of his energy to relieving his father of the burdens of rule, making sure he had the best medical attention available and refusing to believe that one day his father would not be there. So, if Hassan was using words like 'failing', then the old man's health must indeed be grave.

'What happened?' She began to walk towards him. 'I thought the last treatment was—'

'Your interest is a little too late in coming,' Hassan cut in, and with a flick of a hand halted her steps. 'For I don't recall you showing any concern about what it would do to his health when you left a year ago.'

That wasn't fair, and Leona blinked as his words pricked a tender part of her. Sheikh Khalifa was a good man—a kind man. They had become strong, close friends while she had lived at the palace. 'He understood why I felt I needed to leave,' she responded painfully.

You think so? Hassan's cynical expression derided. 'Well, I did not,' he said out loud. 'But, since you decided it was the right thing for you to do, I now have a serious problem on my hands. For I am, in effect, deemed weak for allowing my wife to walk away from me, and my critics are making rumbling noises about the stability of the country if I do not display some leadership.'

'So you decided to show that leadership by abducting me, then dragging me back to Rahman?' Her thick laugh poured scorn over that suggestion, because they both knew taking her back home had to be the worst thing Hassan could possibly do to prove that particular point.

'You would prefer that I take this second wife who makes you flee in pain when the subject appears in front of you?'

'She is what you need, not me.' It almost choked her to say the words. But they were dealing with the truth here, painful though that truth may be. And the truth was that she was no longer the right wife for the heir to a sheikhdom.

'I have the wife I want,' he answered grimly.

'But not the wife you *need*, Hassan!' she countered wretchedly.

His eyes flicked up to clash with her eyes. 'Is that your way of telling me that you no longer love me?' he challenged.

Oh, dear God. Lifting a trembling hand up to cover her eyes, Leona gave a shake of her head in refusal to answer. Without warning Hassan was suddenly moving at speed down the length of the room.

'Answer me!' he insisted when he came to a stop in front of her.

Swallowing on a lump of tears, Leona turned her face away. 'Yes,' she whispered.

His sudden grip on her hand dragged it from her eyes. 'To my face,' he instructed, 'You will tell me this to my face!'

Her head whipped up, tear darkened eyes fixing painfully on burning black. 'Don't—' she pleaded.

But he was not going to give in. He was pale and he was hurt and he was furiously angry. 'I want to hear you state that you feel no love for me,' he persisted. 'I want you to tell that wicked lie to my face. And then I want to hear you beg forgiveness when I prove to you otherwise! Do you understand, Leona?'

'All right! So, I love you! Does that make it all okay?' she cried out. 'I love you but I will not stay married to you! I will *not* watch you ruin your life because of me!'

There—it was out. The bitter truth. On voicing it, she broke free and reeled away, hurting so much it was almost impossible to breathe. 'And your life?' he persisted relentlessly. 'What happens to it while you play the sacrificial lamb for mine?'

'I'll get by,' she said, trying to walk on legs that were shaking so badly she wasn't sure if she was going to fall down.

'You'll marry again?'

She shuddered and didn't reply.

'Take lovers in an attempt to supplant me?'

Harsh and cruel though he sounded, she could hear his anguish. 'I need no one,' she whispered.

'Then you mean to spend the rest of your life watching me produce progeny with this second wife I am to take?'

'Oh, dear heaven.' She swung around. 'What are you trying to do to me?' she choked out tormentedly.

'Make you see,' he gritted. 'Make you open your eyes and *see* what it is you are condemning us both to.'

'But I'm not condemning you to anything! I am giving you my blessing to do what you want with your life!'

If she'd offered to give him a whole harem he could not have been more infuriated. His face became a map of hard angles. 'Then I will take what I want!' It was a declaration of intent that propelled him across the space between them. Before Leona knew what was coming she was locked in his arms and being lifted until their eyes were level. Startled green irises locked with burning black passion. He gave her one small second to read their message before he was kissing her furiously. Shocked out of one kind of torment, she found herself flung into the middle of another—because once again she had no will to fight. She even released a protesting groan when her feet found solid ground again and he broke the urgent kiss.

Her lips felt hot, and pulsed with such a telling fullness that she had to lick them to try and cool them down. His breath left his body on a hiss that brought her eyes flickering dazedly up to his. Thick dark lashes rested over ebony eyes that were fixed on the moist pink tip of her tongue. A slither of excitement skittered right down the front of her. Her breasts grew tight, her abdomen warming at the prospect of what all of this meant.

Making love. Feeling him deep inside her. No excuses, no drawing back this time. She only had to look at Hassan to know this was it. He was about to stake his claim on what belonged to him.

'You will regret this later,' she warned unsteadily, because she knew how his passions and his conscience did not always walk in tandem—especially not where she was concerned.

'Are you denying me?' he threw back in a voice that said he was interested in the answer, but only out of curiosity.

Well, Leona asked herself, are you?

The answer was no, she was not denying him anything he wanted to take from her tonight. Tomorrow was another day, another war, another set of agonising conflicts. Reaching up, she touched a gentle finger to his mouth, drew its shape, softened the tension out of it, then sighed, went up on tiptoe and gently joined their mouths.

His hands found the slender frame of her hips and drew her against him; her hands lifted higher to link around his neck so her fingers could slide sensually into his silk dark hair. It was an embrace that sank them into a long deep loving. Her dress fell away, slithering down her body on a pleasurable whisper of silk against flesh. Beneath she wore a dark gold lace bra, matching high-leg briefs and lace-topped stockings. Hassan discovered all of this with the sensual stroke of long fingers. He knew each pleasure point, the quality of each little gasp she breathed into his mouth. When her bra fell away, she sighed and pressed herself against him; when his fingers slid beneath the briefs to cup her bottom she allowed him to ease her into closer contact. They knew each other, *loved* each other—cared so very deeply about each other. Fight they might do—often. They might have insurmountable problems. But nothing took away the love and caring. It was there, as much part of them as the life-giving oxygen they took into their lungs.

'You want me,' he declared.

'I've always wanted you,' she sadly replied.

'I am your other half.'

And I am your broken one, Leona thought, releasing an achingly melancholy sigh.

Maybe he knew what she was thinking, because his mouth took burning possession that gave no more room to think at all. It came as an unwelcome break when he lowered her down onto the bed then straightened, taking her briefs with him. Her love-flooded eyes watched his eyes roam over her. He was no longer being driven by his inner devils, she realised as she watched him removing his own clothing. Her compliance had neutralised the compelling need to stake his claim.

So she watched him follow her every movement as she made a sensual love-play out of removing her stockings from her long slender legs. His dark robe landed on the floor on top of her clothing; the tunic eventually went the same way. Beneath waited a desert-bronzed silk-smooth torso, with a muscled structure that set her green eyes glowing with pleasure and made her fingers itch to touch. Those muscles rippled and flexed as he reached down to grasp the only piece of clothing he had left to remove. The black shorts trailed away from a sexual force that set her feminine counterpart pulsing with anticipation.

He knew what was happening, smiled a half-smile, then came to lean over her, lowering his raven head to place a kiss there that was really a claim of ownership. She breathed out a shivering breath of pleasure and he was there to claim that also. Then she had all of him covering her. It was the sweetest feeling she had ever experienced. He was her Arabian lover. The man she had seen across a crowded room long years ago. And she had never seen another man clearly since.

He seduced her mouth, he seduced her body, he seduced her into seducing him. When it all became too much without deeper contact, he eased himself between her thighs and slowly joined them.

Her responsive groan made him pause. 'What?' he questioned anxiously.

'I've missed you so much.' She sighed the words out helplessly.

It was a catalyst that sent him toppling. He staked his claim on those few emotive words with every driving thrust. She died a little. It was strange how she did that, she found herself thinking as the pleasure began to run like liquid fire. They came as one, within the grip of hard, gasping shudders and afterwards lay still, locked together, as their bodies went through the pleasurable throes of settling back down again.

Then nothing moved, not their bodies nor even their quiet breathing. The silence came—pure, numbing, unbreakable silence.

Why?

Because it had all been so beautiful but also so very empty. And nothing was ever going to change that.

Hassan moved first, levering himself away to land on his feet by the bed. He didn't even spare her a glance as he walked away. Sensational naked, smooth and sleek, he touched a finger to the wall and a cleverly concealed door sprung open. As he stepped through it Leona caught a glimpse of white tiling and realised it was a bathroom. Then the door closed, shutting him in and her completely out.

Closing her eyes, she lifted an arm up to cover them, and pressed her lips together to stop them from trembling on the tears she was having to fight. For this was not a new situation she was dealing with here. It had happened before—often—and was just one of the many reasons why she had left him in the end. The pain had been too great to go on taking it time after time. His pain, her pain—she had never been able to distinguish where one ended and the other began. The only difference here tonight was that she'd somehow managed to let herself forget that, until this cold, solitary moment.

Hassan stood beneath the pulsing jet of the power shower and wanted to hit something so badly that he had to brace his hands against the tiles and lock every muscle to keep the murderous feeling in. His body was replete but his heart was grinding against his ribcage with a frustration that nothing could cure.

Silence. He hated that silence. He hated knowing he had nothing worth saying with which to fill it in. And he still had to go back in there and face it. Face the dragging sense of his own helplessness and—worse—he had to face hers.

His wife. His woman. The other half of him. Head lowered so the water sluiced onto his shoulders and down his back, he tried to predict what her next move was going to be, and came up with only one grim answer. She was not going to stay. He could bully her as much as he liked, but in the end she was still going to walk away from him unless he could come up with something important enough to make her stay.

Maybe he should have used more of his father's illness, he told himself. A man she loved, a man she'd used to spend hours of every day with, talking, playing board games or just quietly reading to him when he was too weak to enjoy anything else.

But his father had not been enough to make her want to

stay the last time. The old fool had given her his blessing, had missed her terribly, yet even on the day he'd gone to see him before he left the palace he had still maintained that Leona had had to do what she'd believed was right.

So who was in the wrong here? Him for wanting to spend his life with one particular woman, or Leona for wanting to do what was right?

He hated that phrase, *doing what was right*. It reeked of duty at the expense of everything: duty to his family, duty to his country, duty to produce the next Al-Qadim son and heir.

Well, I don't need a son. I don't need a second wife to produce one for me like some specially selected brood mare! I need a beautiful red-haired creature who makes my heart ache each time I look at her. I *don't* need to see that glazed look of emptiness she wears after we make love!

On a sigh he turned round, swapped braced hands for braced shoulders against the shower wall. The water hit his face and stopped him breathing. He didn't care if he never breathed again—until instinct took over from grim stubbornness and forced him to move again.

Coming out of the bathroom a few minutes later, he had to scan the room before he spotted her sitting curled up in one of the chairs. She had opened the curtains and was just sitting there staring out, with her wonderful hair gleaming hot against the pale damask upholstery. She had wrapped herself in a swathe of white and a glance at the tumbled bed told him she had dragged free the sheet of Egyptian cotton to wear.

His gaze dropped to the floor by the bed, where their clothes still lay in an intimate huddle that was a lot more honest than the two of them were with each other.

'Find out how Ethan is.'

The sound of her voice brought his attention back to her. She hadn't moved, had not turned to look at him, and the demand spoke volumes as to what was really being said. Barter and exchange. She had given him more of herself than she had intended to do; now she wanted something back by return.

Without a word he crossed to the internal telephone and found out what she wanted to know, ordered some food to be sent in to them, then strode across the room to sit down in the chair next to hers. 'He caught an accidental blow to the jaw which knocked him out for a minute or two, but he is fine now,' he assured her. 'And is dining with Rafiq as we speak.'

'So he wasn't part of this great plan of abduction you plotted with my father.' It wasn't a question, it was a sign of relief.

'I am devious and underhand on occasion but not quite that devious and underhand,' he countered dryly.

Her chin was resting on her bent knees, but she turned her head to look at him through dark, dark eyes. Her hair flowed across her white-swathed shoulders, and her soft mouth looked vulnerable enough to conquer in one smooth swoop. His body quickened, temptation clawing across flesh hidden beneath his short robe of sand-coloured silk.

'Convincing my own father to plot against me wasn't devious or underhand?' she questioned.

'He was relieved I was ready to break the deadlock,' he informed her. 'He wished me well, then offered me all the help he could give.'

Her lack of comment was one in itself. Her following sigh punctuated it. She was seeing betrayal from her own father, but it just was not true. 'You knew he worried about you,' he inserted huskily. 'Yet you didn't tell him why you left me, did you?'

The remark lost him contact with her eyes as she turned them frontward again, and the way she stared out into the inky blackness beyond the window closed up his throat, because he knew what she was really seeing as she looked out there.

'Coming to terms with being a failure is not something I wanted to share with anyone,' she murmured dully.

'You are not a failure,' he denied.

'I am infertile!' She flashed out the one word neither of them wanted to hear.

It launched Hassan to his feet on a surge of anger. 'You are not infertile!' he ground out harshly. 'That is not what the doctors said, and you know it is not!'

'Will you stop hiding from it?' she cried, scrambling to her feet to stand facing him, with her face as white as the sheet she clutched around her and her eyes as black as the darkness outside. 'I have one defunct ovary and the other one ovulates only when it feels like it!' She spelt it out for him.

'Which does not add up to infertility,' he countered forcefully.

'After all of these years of nothing, you can still bring yourself to say that?'

She was staring up at him as if he was deliberately trying to hurt her. And, because he had no answer to that final charge, he had to ask himself if that had been his subconscious intention. The last year had been hell to live through and the year preceding only marginally better. Married life had become a place in which they'd walked with the darkness of disappointment shadowing their past and future. In the end, Leona had not been able to take it any more so she'd left him. If she wanted to know what failure really felt like then she should have trodden in his shoes as he'd battled with his own failure to relieve this woman he loved of the heavy burden she was forced to carry.

'We will try other methods of conception,' he stated grimly.

If it was possible her face went even whiter. 'My eggs harvested like grains of wheat and your son conceived in a test tube? Your people would never forgive me for putting you through such an indignity, and those who keep the Al-Qadim family in power will view the whole process with deep suspicion.'

Her voice had begun to wobble. His own throat closed on

the need to swallow, because she was right, though he did not want her to be. For she was talking about the old ones, those tribal leaders of the desert who really maintained the balance of power in Rahman. They lived by the old ways and regarded anything remotely modern as necessary evil to be embraced only if all other sources had been exhausted. Hassan had taken a big risk when he'd married a western woman. The old ones had surprised him by deciding to see his decision to do so as a sign of strength. But that had been the only concession they had offered him with regard to his choice of wife. For why go to such extremes to father a son he could conceive as easily by taking a second wife?

Which was why this subject had always been so sensitive, and why Leona suddenly shook her head and said, 'Oh, why did you have to bring me back here?' Then she turned and walked quickly away from him, making unerringly for the bathroom he had so recently used for the same purpose—to be alone with her pain.

CHAPTER FOUR

Two hours, Leona noticed, as she removed her slender gold watch from her wrist with badly trembling fingers and laid it on the marble surface along with the diamonds from her ears and throat. Two hours together and already they were tearing each other to pieces.

On a sigh she swivelled round to sink down onto the toilet seat and stare dully at her surroundings. White. Everything was white. White-tiled walls and floor, white ceramics—even the sheet she had discarded lay in a soft white heap on the floor. The room needed a bit of colour to add some—

She stopped herself right there, closing her eyes on the knowledge that she had slipped into professional mode and knowing she had done it to escape from what she should really be thinking about.

This situation, this mad, foolish, heart-flaying situation, which was also so bitter-sweet and special. She didn't know whether to laugh at Hassan's outrageous method of bringing them together, or sob at the unnecessary agony he was causing the both of them.

In the end she did both, released a laugh that turned into a sob and buried the sound in her hands. Each look, each touch, was an act of love that bound them together. Each word, each thought, was an act of pain that tore them apart at the seams.

Then she remembered his face when he had made the ultimate sacrifice. Chin up, face carved, mouth so flat it was hardly a mouth any more. When the man had had to turn himself into a prince before he could utter the words, 'We will try other methods of conception,' she had known they had nothing left to fight for.

What was she supposed to have done? Made the reciprocal sacrifice to their love and offered to remain his first wife while he took a second? She just could not do it, could not live with the agony of knowing that when he wasn't in her bed he would be lying in another. The very idea was enough to set her insides curling up in pained dismay while her covered eyes caught nightmare visions of him trying to be fair, trying to pretend it wasn't really happening, that he wasn't over the moon when the new wife conceived his first child. How long after that before his love began to shift from her to this other woman with whom he could relax—enjoy her without feeling pain every time he looked at her?

'No,' she whispered. 'Stop it.' She began to shiver. It just wasn't even an option, so she must stop thinking about it! He knew that—he *knew it*! It was why he had taunted her with the suggestion earlier. He had been angry and had gone for the jugular and had enjoyed watching her die in front of him! It had always been like this: exploding flashes of anger and frustration, followed by wild leaps into sensual forgetfulness, followed by the low-of-low moments when neither could even look at the other because the empty truth was always still waiting there for them to re-emerge.

Empty.

On a groan she stood up, and groaned again as tiny muscles all over her body protested at being forced into movement. The fall, the lovemaking, or just the sheer stress of it all? she wondered, then wearily supposed it was a combination of all three.

So why do it? Why put them both back into a situation they had played so many times before it was wretched? Or was that it? she then thought on a sudden chill that shot down her backbone. Had he needed to play out the scene this one last time before he could finally accept that their marriage was over?

Sick. She felt sick. On trembling legs she headed quickly for the shower cubicle and switched the jet on so water sluiced over her body. Duty. It was all down to duty. His duty to produce an heir, her duty to let him. With any other man the love would be enough; those *other methods of conception* would be made bearable by the strength of that love. But she'd fallen in love with a prince not a man. And the prince had fallen in love with a barren woman.

Barren. How ugly that word was. How cold and bitter and horribly cheap. For there was nothing barren about the way she was feeling, nor did those feelings come cheap. They cost her a part of herself each time she experienced them. Like now, as they ate away at her insides until it was all she could do to slide down into a pathetic huddle in the corner of the shower cubicle and wait for it all to recede.

Where was she? What was she doing in there? She had been shut inside the bathroom for half an hour, and with a glance at his watch, Hassan continued to pace the floor on the vow that if she didn't come out in two minutes he was going in there after her.

None of this—*none* of it—was going the way he had planned it. How had he managed to trick himself into diluting just how deep their emotions ran, how painful the whole thing was going to be? He hit his brow with the palm of his hand, then uttered a few choice curses at his arrogant belief that all he'd needed to do was hook her up and haul her back in for the rest to fall into place around them.

All he'd wanted to do was make sure she was safe, back here where she belonged, no matter what the problems. So instead he'd scared the life out of her, almost lost her to the depths of the ocean, fought like the devil over issues that were so old they did not need raking over! He'd even lied to score points, had watched her run in a flood of tears, watched her fly through the air down a set of stairs he now wished had never been put there. Shocked, winded and dazed by the whole crazy situation, he had then committed his worst sin and had ravished her. Now she had locked herself away behind a bathroom door because she could not deal with him daring to make an offer they both knew was not, and never had been, a real option!

What was left? Did he unsheath his ceremonial scabbard and offer to finish them both off like two tragic lovers?

Oh, may Allah forgive him, he prayed as his blood ran cold and he leapt towards the bathroom door. She wouldn't. She was made of stronger stuff, he told himself as he lifted a clenched fist to bang on the door just as it came open.

She was wearing only a towel and her hair was wet, slicked to her beautiful head like a ruby satin veil. Momentarily shocked by the unexpected face-to-face confrontation, they both just stared at each other. Then he bit out, 'Are you all right?'

'Of course,' she replied. 'Why shouldn't I be?'

He had no answer to offer that did not sound insane, so he took another way out and reached for her, pulled her into his arms and kissed her—hard. By the time he let her up for air again she was breathless.

'Hassan—'

'No,' he interrupted. 'We have talked enough for one night.'

Turning away, he went over to the bed to retrieve the pearl-white silk robe he had laid out ready for her. During her absence the room had been returned to its natural neatness, at his instruction, and a table had been laid for dinner in the centre, with the food waiting for them on a heated trolley standing beside it.

He saw her eyes taking all of this in as he walked back to where she was standing. She also noticed that the lights had been turned down and candles had been lit on the table. She was no fool; she knew he had set the scene with a second seduction in mind and he didn't bother to deny it.

'Here,' he said, and opened the robe up between his hands, inviting her to slip into it.

There was a pause where she kept her eyes hidden beneath the sweep of her dusky lashes. She was trying to decide how to deal with this and he waited in silence, more than willing to let the decision be hers after having spent the previous few minutes listing every other wrong move he had made until now.

'Just for tonight,' she said, and lifted those lashes to show him the firmness of that decision. 'Tomorrow you take me back to San Estéban.'

His mouth flexed as the urge to say, Never, throbbed on the end of his tongue. 'Tomorrow we—talk about it,' he offered as his only compromise, though he knew it was no compromise at all and wondered if she knew it too.

He suspected she did, suspected she knew he had not gone to all of this trouble just to snatch a single night with her. But those wonderful lashes fluttered down again. Her soft mouth, still pulsing from his kiss, closed over words she decided not to say, and with only a nod of her head she lost the towel, stepped forward and turned to allow him to help feed her arms into the kimono-type sleeves of the robe.

It was a concession he knew he did not deserve. A concession he wanted to repay with a kiss of another kind, where bodies met and senses took over. Instead, he turned her to face him, smoothed his fingers down the robe's silken border from slender shoulders to narrow waist, then reached for the belt and tied it for her.

His gentle ministrations brought a reluctant smile to her lips. 'The calm before the storm,' she likened dryly.

'Better this than what I really want to do,' he very ruefully replied.

'You mean this?' she asked, and lifted her eyes to his to let him see what was running through her head, then reached up and kissed him, before drawing away again with a very mocking smile.

As she turned to walk towards the food trolley she managed to trail her fingers over that part of him that was already so hard it was almost an embarrassment. The little vixen. He released a soft laugh. She might appear subdued on the surface, but underneath she still possessed enough spirit to play the tease.

They ate poached salmon on a bed of spinach, and beef stroganoff laden with cream. Hassan kept her glass filled with the crisp dry white wine she liked, while he drank sparkling water. As the wine helped mellow her mood some more, Leona managed to completely convince herself that all she wanted was this one wonderful night and she was prepared to live on it for ever. By the time the meal was finished and he suggested a walk on the deck, she was happy to go with him.

Outside the air was warm and as silken as the darkness that surrounded them. Both in bare feet, dressed only in their robes, they strolled along the deck and could have been the only two people on board it was so quiet and deserted.

'Rafiq is entertaining Ethan—up there,' Hassan explained when she asked where everyone else was. Following his gaze, Leona could see lights were burning in the windows of the deck above.

'Should we be joining them?'

'I don't think they would appreciate the interruption,' he drawled. 'They have a poker game planned with several members of the crew, and our presence would dampen their—enthusiasm.'

Which was really him saying he didn't want to share her with anyone. 'You have an answer for everything, don't you?' she murmured.

'I try.' He smiled.

It was a slaying smile that sent the heat of anticipation burning between the cradle of her hip-bones, forcing her to look away so he wouldn't see just how susceptible she was even to his smile. Going to lean against the yacht's rail, she looked down to watch the white horses chase along the dark blue hull of the boat. They were moving at speed, slicing through the water on slick silent power that made her wonder how far they were away from San Estéban by now.

She didn't ask, though, because it was the kind of question that could start a war. 'This is one very impressive toy, even for an oil-rich sheikh,' she remarked.

'One hundred and ninety feet in length,' he announced, and came to lean beside her with his back against the rail. 'Twenty-nine feet across the beam.' His arm slid around her waist and twisted her to stand in front of him so she could follow his hand as he pointed. 'The top deck belongs mainly to the control room, where my very efficient captain keeps a smoothly running ship,' he said. 'The next down belongs to the sun deck and main reception salons designed to suitably luxurious standards for entertaining purposes. We stand upon what is known as the shade deck, it being cast mostly in the shade of the deck above,' he continued, so smoothly that she laughed because she knew he was really mocking the whole sumptuous thing. 'One half is reserved for our own personal use, with our private staterooms, my private offices etcetera,' he explained, 'while the other half is split equally between outer sun deck, outer shade deck, plus some less formal living space.'

'Gosh, you're so lucky to be this rich.' She sighed.

'And I haven't yet finished this glorious tour,' he replied. 'For below our feet lies the cabin deck, complete with six private suites easily fit for the occupation of kings. Then there is the engine room and crew's quarters below that. We can also offer a plunge pool, gymnasium and an assortment of nautical toys to make our weary lot a happier one.'

'Does it have a name, this sheikh's floating palace?' she enquired laughingly.

'Mmm. *Sexy Lady*,' he growled, and lowered his head so he could bury his teeth in the side of her neck where it met her shoulder.

'You're joking!' she accused, turning round in his arms to stare at him.

'Okay.' He shrugged. 'I am joking.'

'Then what is she called?' she demanded, as her heart skipped a beat then stopped altogether because he looked so wonderful standing here with his lean dark features relaxed and smiling naturally for the first time. She loved him quite desperately—how could she not? He was her—

The laughter suddenly died on her lips, his expression telling her something she didn't want to believe. 'No,' she breathed in denial. He couldn't have done—he *wouldn't*…

'Why not?' he challenged softly.

'Not in this case!' she snapped at him, not knowing quite what it was that was upsetting her. But upset she was; her eyes felt too hot, her chest too tight, and she had a horrible feeling she was about to weep all over his big hard beautiful chest!

'It is traditional to name a boat after your most cherished loved-one,' he pointed out. 'And why am I defending myself when I could not have paid you a better compliment than this?'

'Because…' she began shakily.

'You don't like it,' he finished for her.

'No!' she confirmed, then almost instantly changed her mind and said. 'Yes, I like it! But you shouldn't have! Y-you—'

His mouth crushed the rest of her protest into absolute oblivion, which was where it belonged anyway, because she didn't know what she was saying, only that a warm sweet wave of love was crashing over her and it was so dangerously seductive that—

She fell into it. She just let the wave close over her head and let him drown her in the heat of his passion, the power of his arms and the hunger of his kiss.

'Bed?' he suggested against her clinging mouth.

'Yes,' she agreed, then fed her fingers into his hair and her tongue between his ready lips. A groan broke low in his throat; it was husky and gorgeous; she tasted it greedily. A hand that knew her so very well curved over her thighs, slid up beneath her wrap, then cupped her bottom so he could bring her into closer contact with his desire. It was all very hot and very hungry. With a flick of a few scraps of silk they could be making love right here against the yacht's rail and in front of however many unseen eyes that happened to be glancing this way.

Hassan must have been thinking similarly because he suddenly put her from him. 'Bed,' he repeated, two dark streaks of colour accentuating his cheekbones and the fevered glitter in his eyes. 'Can you walk, or do I carry you?'

'I can run,' she informed him candidly, and grabbed hold of his hand, then turned to stride off on long slender legs with his husky laugh following as she pulled him behind her.

Back in their stateroom, now magically cleared of all evidence that they had eaten, they parted at the end of the bed, one stepping to one side of it, one to the other. Eyes locking in a needle-sharp, sensual love game, they disrobed together, climbed into the bed together and came together.

Hot, slow and deep, they made love into the night and didn't have to worry about empty spaces in between because one loving simply merged into another until—finally—they slept in each other's arms, legs entwined and faces so close on the pillows that the sleep was almost a long kiss in itself.

Leona came awake to find the place beside her in the bed empty and felt disappointment tug at her insides. For a while she just lay there, watching the sunlight seeping in through the window slowly creep towards her across the room, and tried not to let her mind open up to what it was bringing with it.

After a night built on fantasy had to come reality, not warm, like the sun, but cold, like the shadow she could already feel descending upon her even as she tried to hold it back for a little while longer.

A sound caught her attention. Moving her head just a little, she watched Hassan walk out of the bathroom wearing only a towel, his sun-brown skin fashioned to look almost like skillfully tanned leather. For such a dark man he was surprisingly free of body hair, which meant she could watch unhindered each beautifully toned muscle as he strode across to one of the concealed doors in the wall and sprung it open at a touch to reveal a wardrobe to provide for the man who had everything. A drawer was opened and he selected a pair of white cotton undershorts, dropped the towel to give her a glimpse of lean tight buttocks before he pulled the shorts on. A pair of stone-washed outer shorts followed. Zipped and buttoned, they rested low on a waist that did not know the meaning of spare flesh to spoil his sleek appearance. A casual shirt came next, made of such fine white Indian cotton she could still see the outline of his body through it.

'I can feel you watching me,' he remarked without turning.

'I like to look at you,' Leona replied. And she did; rightly or wrongly in their present situation, he was a man to watch whatever he was doing, even fastening buttons as he was doing now.

Shirt cuffs left open, he turned to walk towards the bed. The closer he came the faster her heart decided to beat. 'I like to look at you, too,' he murmured, bracing his hands on either side of head so he could lean down and kiss her.

He smelt clean and fresh and his face wore the smooth sheen of a wet razor shave. Her lips clung to his, because she was still pretending, and her arms reached up so she could clasp them round the back of his neck. 'Come back to bed with me,' she invited.

'So that you can ravish me? No way,' he refused. 'As the wise ones will tell you, my darling, too much of a good thing is bad for you.'

He kissed her again to soften the refusal, and his mouth was smiling as he straightened away, but as his hands reached up to gently remove her hands she saw the toughening happening behind his eyes. Hassan had already made contact with reality, she realised.

With that he turned away and strode back to the wall to spring open another set of doors which revealed clothes for the woman who wanted for nothing—except her man. And already she felt as if he had moved right out of her reach.

'Get up and get dressed,' he instructed as he walked towards the door. 'Breakfast will be served on the sun deck in fifteen minutes.'

As she watched him reach for the door handle the shadow

of reality sank that bit deeper into her skin. 'Nothing has changed, Hassan,' she told him quietly. 'When I leave this room I won't be coming back to it again.'

He paused, but he did not turn to glance back at her. 'Everything has changed,' he countered grimly. 'You are back where you belong. This room is only part of that.' Then he was gone, giving her no chance to argue.

Leona returned to watching the sun inch its way across the cream carpet for a while. Then, on a sigh, she slid out of the bed and went to get herself ready to face the next round of argument.

In another room not that far away Hassan was facing up to a different opponent. Ethan Hayes was standing there in the clothes he had arrived in minus the bow tie, and he was angry. In truth Hassan didn't blame him. He was wearing a bruise on his jaw that would appal Leona if she saw it, and he had a thick head through being encouraged to imbibe too much alcohol the night before.

'What made you pull such a crazy stunt?' he was demanding.

Since Hassan had been asking himself the same thing, he now found himself short of an adequate answer. 'I apologise for my men,' he said. 'Their…enthusiasm for the task got the better of them, I am afraid.'

'You can say that again.' Ethan touched his bruised jaw. 'I was out for the count for ten minutes! The next thing I know I am stuck on a yacht I don't want to be on, and Leona is nowhere to be seen!'

'She's worried about you, too, if that is any consolation.'

'No, it damn well isn't,' Ethan said toughly. 'What the hell was wrong with making contact by conventional methods? You scared the life out of her, not to mention the life out of me.'

'I know, and I apologise again.' Not being a man born to be conciliatory, being forced to be so now was beginning to grate, and his next cool remark reflected that. 'Let it be said that you will be generously compensated for the... disruption.'

Ethan Hayes stiffened in violent offence. 'I don't want compensation,' he snapped. 'I want to see for myself that Leona is okay!'

'Are you daring to imply that I could harm my wife?'

'I don't know, do I?' Ethan returned in a tone deliberately aimed to provoke. 'Overenthusiasm can be infectious.'

Neither man liked the other, though it was very rare that either came out from behind their polite masks to reveal it. But, as the sparks began to fly between the two of them, this meeting was at risk of being one of those times. Leona might prefer to believe that Ethan Hayes was not in love with her. But, as a man very intimate with the symptoms, Hassan knew otherwise. The passion with which he spoke her name, the burn that appeared in his eyes, and the inherent desire to protect her from harm all made Ethan Hayes' feelings plain. And, as far as Hassan was concerned, the handsome Englishman's only saving grace was the deep sense of honour that made him respect the wedding ring Leona wore.

But knowing this did not mean that Hassan could dismiss the other man's ability to turn her towards him if he really set his mind to it. He had the build and the looks to turn any woman's head.

Was he really afraid of that happening? he then asked himself, and was disturbed to realise that, yes, he was afraid. Always had been, always would be, he admitted, as he fought to maintain his polite mask because, at this juncture, he needed Ethan Hayes' cooperation if he was going to get him off this boat before Leona could reach him.

So, on a sigh which announced his withdrawal from the threatening confrontation, he said grimly, 'Time is of the essence,' and went on to explain to the other man just enough of the truth to grab his concern.

'A plot to get rid of her?' Ethan was shocked and Hassan could not blame him for being so.

'A plot to use her as a lever to make me concede to certain

issues they desire from me,' he amended. 'I am still holding onto the belief that they did not want to turn this into an international incident by harming her in any way.'

'Just snatching her could do it,' Ethan pointed out.

'Only if it became public property,' Hassan responded. 'They would be betting on Victor and myself holding our silence out of fear for Leona's safety.'

'Does she know?' Ethan asked.

'Not yet,' Hassan confessed. 'And not at all if I can possibly get away with it.'

'So why does she think she's here?'

'Why do you think?' Hassan countered, and gained some enjoyment out of watching Ethan stiffen as he absorbed the full masculine depth of his meaning. 'As long as she remains under my protection no one can touch her.'

Ethan's response took him by surprise because he dared to laugh. 'You've no chance, Hassan,' he waged. 'Leona will fight you to the edge and back before she will just sit down and do what you want her to do simply because you've decided that is how it must be.'

'Which is why I need your support in this,' Hassan replied. 'I need you to leave this boat before she can have an opportunity to use your departure as an excuse to jump ship with you.'

He got it. In the end, and after a bit more wrangling, he watched Ethan Hayes turn to the door on a reluctant agreement to go. And, oddly, Hassan admired him for trusting him enough to do this, bearing in mind the year that had gone before.

'Don't hurt her again.' Almost as if he could read his thoughts, Ethan issued that gruff warning right on cue.

'My wife's well-being is and always has been of paramount importance to me,' Hassan responded in a decidedly cooler tone.

Ethan turned, looked him directly in the eye, and for once the truth was placed in the open. 'You hurt her a year ago. A man gets only one chance at doing that.'

The kid gloves came off. Hassan's eyes began to glint. 'Take a small piece of advice,' he urged, 'and do not presume to understand a marital relationship until you have tried it for yourself.'

'I know a broken-hearted woman when I see one,' Ethan persisted.

'And has she been any less broken-hearted in the year we have been apart?'

Game, set and match, Hassan recognised, as the other man conceded that final point to him, and with just a nod of his head Ethan went out of the door and into the capable hands of the waiting Rafiq.

At about the same time that Rafiq was escorting Ethan to the waiting launch presently tied up against the side of the yacht, Leona was slipping her arms into the sleeves of a white linen jacket that matched the white linen trousers she had chosen to wear. Beneath the jacket she wore a pale green sun top, and she had contained her hair in a simple pony-tail tied up with a green silk scarf. As she turned towards the door she decided that if she managed to ignore the throbbing ache happening inside her then she was as ready as she ever could be for the battle she knew was to come with Hassan.

Stepping out of the stateroom, the first person she saw was a bearded man dressed in a long white tunic and the usual white *gutrah* on his head.

'Faysal!' Her surprise was clear, her smile warm. Faysal responded by pressing his palms together and dipping into the kind of low bow that irritated Hassan but didn't bother Leona at all simply because she ignored it. 'I didn't know you were here on the boat. Are you well?' she enquired as she walked towards him.

'I am very well, my lady,' he confirmed, but beneath the beard she had a suspicion he was blushing uncomfortably at the informal intimacy she was showing him.

'And your wife?' she asked gently.

'Oh, she is very well,' he confirmed with a distinct soft-

ening in his formal tone. 'The—er—problem she suffered
has gone completely. We are most grateful to you for taking
the trouble to ensure she was treated by the best people.'

'I didn't do anything but point her in the right direction,
Faysal.' Leona smiled. 'I am only grateful that she felt she
could confide in me.'

'You saved her life.'

'Many people saved her life.' Daring his affront, she
crossed the invisible line Arab males drew between themselves and females and reached out to press her hands against
the backs of his hands. 'But you and I were good conspira-
tors, hmm, Faysal?'

'Indisputably, my lady.' His mouth almost cracked into a
smile but he was too stressed at having her hands on his, and
in the end she relented and moved away.

'If you would come this way…' he bowed '…I am to
escort you to my lord Hassan.'

Ah, my lord Hassan, Leona thought, and felt her lighter
mood drop again as Faysal indicated that she precede him
down the steps she had taken a tumble on the night before.
On the other side of the foyer was a staircase which Leona
presumed led up to the deck above.

With Faysal tracking two steps behind her, she made her
way up and into the sunlight flooding the upper deck, where
she paused to take a look around. The sky was a pure, un-
interrupted blue and the sea the colour of turquoise. The sun
was already hot on her face and she had to shade her eyes
against the way it was reflecting so brightly off the white
paintwork of the boat.

'You managed to make Faysal blush, I see,' a deep voice
drawled lazily.

Turning about, she found that Faysal had already melted
away, as was his habit, and that Hassan was sitting at a table
laid for breakfast beneath the shade of a huge white canvas
awning, studying her through slightly mocking eyes. Her
heart tried to leap in her breast but she refused to let it.

'There is a real human being hiding behind all of that strict protocol, if you would only look and see him.'

'The protocol is not my invention. It took generations of family tradition to make Faysal the man he is today.'

'He worships you like a god.'

'And you as his angel of mercy.'

'At least he felt I was approachable enough that he could bring his concerns to me.'

'After I had gently suggested it was what he should do.'

'Oh,' she said; she hadn't realised that.

'Come out of the sun before you burn.'

It was hot, and he was right, but Leona felt safer keeping her distance. She had things to say, and she began with the one subject guaranteed to alter his mellow mood into something else entirely. 'I was hoping that Ethan would be here with you,' she said. 'Since he isn't, I think I will go and look for him.'

Like a sign from Allah that today was not going to be a good day, at that moment the launch powered up and slipped its ties to the yacht.

Attention distracted, Leona glanced over the side, then went perfectly still.

Hassan knew what she was seeing even before he got up to go and join her. Sure enough, there was Ethan standing on the back of the launch. As the small boat began to pick up speed he glanced up, saw them and waved a farewell.

'Wave back, my darling,' he urged smoothly. 'The man will appreciate the assurance that all is well.'

'You rat,' she whispered.

'Of the desert,' he dryly replied, then compounded his sins by bringing an arm to rest across her stiff shoulders and lifting his other to wave.

Leona waved also, he admired her for that because it showed that, despite how angry she was feeling, she was— as always—keeping true to her unfailing loyalty to him.

In the eyes of other people, anyway. He extended that statement as the two of them stood watching Ethan and his passage away from them decrease in size, until the launch was nothing more than an occasional glint amongst many on the ocean. By then Leona was staring beyond the glint, checking the horizon for a glimpse of land that was not there. She was also gripping the rail in front of them with fingers like talons and wishing they were around his throat, he was sure.

'Try to think of it this way,' he suggested. 'I have saved us the trouble of yet another argument.'

CHAPTER FIVE

'WE HAVE to put into port some time,' Leona said coldly. She twisted out from beneath his resting arm then began walking stiffly towards the stairs, so very angry with him that she was quite prepared to lock herself in the stateroom until they did exactly that.

Behind the rigid set of her spine, she heard Hassan release a heavy sigh. 'Come back here,' he instructed. 'I was joking. I know we need to talk.'

But this was no joke, and they both knew it. He was just a ruthless, self-motivated monster, and as far as she was concerned, she had nothing left to— Her thoughts stopped dead. So did her feet when she found her way blocked by a giant of a man with a neat beard and the hawklike features of a desert warrior.

'Well, just look what we have here,' she drawled at this newly arrived target for her anger. 'If it isn't my lord sheikh's fellow conspirator in crime.'

Rafiq had opened his mouth to offer her a greeting, but her tone made him change his mind and instead he dipped into the kind of bow that would have even impressed Faysal, but only managed to sharpen Leona's tongue.

'Don't you dare efface yourself to me when we both know you don't respect me at all,' she sliced at him.

'You are mistaken,' he replied. 'I respect you most deeply.'

'Even while you throw an *abaya* over my head?'

'The *abaya* was an unfortunate necessity,' he explained, 'For you sparkled so brilliantly that you placed us in risk of discovery from the car headlights. Though please accept my apologies if my actions offended you.'

He thought he could mollify her with an apology? 'Do you know what you need, Rafiq Al-Qadim?' she responded. 'You need someone to find you a wife—a real harridan who will make your life such a misery that you won't have time to meddle in mine!'

'You are angry, and rightly so,' he conceded, but his eyes had begun to glint at the very idea of anyone meddling with his life. 'My remorse for the incident with the *abaya* is all yours. Please be assured that if you had toppled into the ocean I would have arrived there ahead of you.'

'But not before me, I think,' another voice intruded. It was very satisfying to hear the impatience in Hassan's tone. He was not a man who liked to be upstaged in any way, which was what Leona had allowed Rafiq to do. 'Leona, come out of the sun,' he instructed. 'Allowing yourself to burn because you are angry is the fool's choice.'

Leona didn't move but Rafiq did. In two strides he was standing right beside her and quite effectively blocking her off from the sun with his impressive shadow.

Which only helped to irritate Hassan all the more. 'Your reason for being up here had better be a good one, Rafiq,' he said grimly.

'Most assuredly,' the other man replied. 'Sheikh Abdul begs an urgent word with you.'

Hassan's smile was thin. 'Worried, is he?'

'Protecting his back,' Rafiq assessed.

'Sheikh Abdul can wait until I have eaten my breakfast.' Levering himself away from the yacht's rail, he walked back to the breakfast table. 'Leona, if you are not over here by the time Rafiq leaves you will not like the consequences.'

'Threats now?' she threw at him.

'Tell the sheikh I will speak to him later,' he said, ignoring her remark to speak to Rafiq.

Rafiq hesitated, stuck between two loyalties and clearly unsure which one to heed. He preferred to stay by Leona's side until she decided to leave the sun, but he also needed to deliver Hassan's message; so a silence dropped and ten-

sion rose. Hassan picked up the coffee pot and poured himself a cup while he waited. He was testing the faith of a man
who had only ever given him his absolute loyalty, and that
surprised and dismayed Leona because, tough and cold
though she knew Hassan could be on occasion, she had never
known him to challenge Rafiq in this way.

In the end she took the pressure off by stepping beneath
the shade of the awning. Rafiq bowed and left. Hassan sent
her a brief smile. 'Thank you,' he said.

'You didn't have to challenge him like that,' she admon-
ished. 'It was an unfair use of your authority.'

'Perhaps,' he conceded. 'But it served its purpose.'

'The purpose of reminding him of his station in life?'

'No, the purpose of making you remember yours.' He
threw her a hard glance. 'We both wield power in our way,
Leona. You have just demonstrated your own by giving
Rafiq the freedom to leave with his pride intact.'

He was right, though she didn't like being forced to realise
it.

'You can be so cruel sometimes.' She released the words
on a sigh. To her surprise Hassan countered it with a laugh.

'You call me cruel when you have just threatened him
with a wife? He has a woman,' he confided, coming to stand
right behind her. 'A black-haired, ruby-eyed, golden-skinned
Spaniard.' Reaching round with his hands, he slipped free
the single button holding her jacket shut, then began to remove the garment. 'She dances the flamenco and famously
turns up men's temperature gauges with her delectably seductive style.' His lips brushed the slender curve of her
newly exposed shoulder. 'But Rafiq assures me that nothing
compares to what she unleashes when she dances only for
him.'

'You've seen her dance?' Before she could stop herself,
Leona had turned her head and given him just what he had
been aiming for, she realised, too late to hide the jealous
green glow in her eyes.

A sleek dark brow arched, dark eyes taunting her with his

answer. 'You like to believe you can set me free but you are really so possessive of me that I can feel the chains tightening, not slackening.'

'And you are so conceited.' She tried to draw back the green eyed monster.

'Because I like the chains?' he quizzed, and further disarmed her.

It wasn't fair, Leona decided; he could seduce her into a mess of confusion in seconds: Ethan, the launch, her sense of righteous indignation at the way she was being manipulated at just about every turn; she was in real danger of becoming lost in the power he had over her. She tried to break free from it. From *her* chains, she recognised.

'I prefer tea to coffee,' she murmured, aiming her concentration at the only neutral thing she could find, which was the table set for breakfast.

The warm sound of his laughter was in recognition of her diversion tactics. Then suddenly he wasn't laughing, he was releasing a gasp of horror. 'You are bruised!' he claimed, sending her gaze flittering to the slight discolouring to her right shoulder that she had noticed herself in the shower earlier.

'It's nothing.' She tried to dismiss it.

But Hassan was already turning her round and his black eyes were hard as they began flashing over every other exposed piece of flesh he could see. 'Me, or the fall?' he demanded harshly.

'The fall, of course.' She frowned, because she couldn't remember a single time in all the years they had been together that Hassan had ever marked her, either in passion or anger, yet he had gone so pale she might have accused him of beating her.

'Any more?' he asked tensely.

'Just my right hip, a little,' she said, holding her tongue about the sore spot at the side of her head, because she could see he wasn't up to dealing with that information. '—Hassan, will you stop it?' she said gasping when he dropped down in front of her and began to unfasten her white trousers. 'It isn't that bad!'

He wasn't listening. The trousers dropped, his fingers were already gently lifting the plain white cotton of her panty line out of the way so he could inspect for himself. 'I am at your feet,' he said in pained apology.

'I can see that,' she replied with a tremor in her voice that had more to do with shock than the humour she'd tried to inject into it. His response was so unnecessary and so very enthralling. 'Just get up now and let me dress,' she pleaded. 'Someone might come, for goodness' sake!'

'Not if they value their necks,' he replied, but at least he began to slide her trousers back over her slender hip-bones.

It had to be the worst bit of timing that Faysal should choose that moment to make one of his silent appearances. Leona was covered—just—but it did not take much imagination for her to know what Faysal must believe he was interrupting. The colour that flooded her cheeks must have aided that impression. Hassan went one further and rose up like a cobra.

'This intrusion had better be worth losing your head for!' he hissed.

For a few awful seconds Leona thought the poor man was going to prostrate himself in an agony of anguish. He made do with a bow to beat all bows. 'My sincerest apologies,' he begged. 'Your most honourable father, Sheikh Khalifa, desires immediate words with you, sir.'

Anyone else and Hassan would have carried out his threat, Leona was sure. Instead his mouth snapped shut, his hands took hold of her and dumped her rudely into a chair.

'Faysal, my wife requires tea.' He shot Leona's own diversion at the other man. Glad of the excuse to go, Faysal almost ran. To Leona he said, 'Eat,' but he wasn't making eye contact, and the two streaks of colour he was wearing on his cheekbones almost made her grin because it was so rare that anyone saw Sheikh Hassan Al-Qadim disconcerted.

'You dare,' he growled, swooping down and kissing her

twitching mouth, then he left quickly with the promise to return in moments.

But moments stretched into minutes. She ate one of the freshly baked rolls a white liveried steward had brought with a pot of tea, then drank the tea—and still Hassan did not return.

Eventually Rafiq appeared with another formal bow and Hassan's apologies. He was engaged in matters of state.

Matters of state she understood having lived before with Hassan disappearing for hours upon end to deal with them.

'Would you mind if I joined you?' Rafiq then requested.

'Orders of state?' she quizzed him dryly.

His half-smile gave her an answer. Her half-smile accompanied her indication to an empty chair. She watched him sit, watched him hunt around for something neutral to say that was not likely to cause another argument. There was no such thing, Leona knew that, so she decided to help him out.

'Tell me about your Spanish mistress,' she invited.

It was the perfect strike back for sins committed against her. Rafiq released a sigh and dragged the *gutrah* from his head, then tossed it aside. This was a familiar gesture for a man of the Al-Qadim household to use. It could convey many things: weariness, anger, contempt or, as in this case, a relayed throwing in of the towel. 'He lacks conscience,' he complained.

'Yet you continue to love him unreservedly, Rafiq, son of Khalifa Al-Qadim,' she quietly replied.

An eyebrow arched. Sometimes, in a certain light, he looked so like Hassan that they could have been twins. But they were not. 'Bastard son,' Rafiq corrected in that proud way of his. 'And you continue to love him yourself, so we had best not throw those particular stones,' he advised.

Rafiq had been born out of wedlock to Sheikh Khalifa's beautiful French mistress, who'd died giving birth to him. The fact that Hassan had only been six months old himself at the time of Rafiq's birth should have made the two half-brothers bitter enemies as they grew up together, one certain of his high place in life, the other just as certain of what would never be his. Yet in truth the two men could not have been closer if they'd shared the same mother. As grown men they had formed a united force behind which their ailing father rested secure in the knowledge that no one would challenge his power while his sons were there to stop them. When Leona came along, she too had been placed within this ring of protection.

Strange, she mused, how she had always been surrounded by strong men for most of her life: her father, Ethan, Rafiq and Hassan; even Sheikh Khalifa, ill though he now was, had always been one of her faithful champions.

'Convince him to let me go,' she requested quietly.

Ebony eyes darkened. 'He had missed you.'

So did green. 'Convince him,' she persisted.

'He was lonely without you.'

This time she had to swallow across the lump those words helped to form in her throat before she could say, 'Please.'

Rafiq leaned across the table, picked up one of her hands and gave it a squeeze. 'Subject over,' he announced very gently.

And it was. Leona could see that. It didn't so much hurt to be stonewalled like this but rather brought it more firmly home to her just how serious Hassan was.

Coming to his feet, Rafiq pulled her up with him. 'Where are we going?' she asked.

'For a tour of the boat in the hopes that the diversion will restrain your desire to weaken my defences.'

'Huh,' she said, for the day had not arrived when anyone could weaken Rafiq in any way involving his beloved brother. But she did not argue the point about needing a diversion.

He turned to collect his *gutrah*. The moment it went back on his head, the other Rafiq reappeared, the proud and remote man. 'If you would be so good as to precede me, my lady. We will collect a hat from your stateroom before we begin…'

Several hours later she was lying on one of the sun loungers on the shade deck, having given in to the heat and changed into a black and white patterned bikini teamed with a cool white muslin shirt. She had been shown almost every room the beautiful yacht possessed, and been formally introduced to Captain Tariq Al-Bahir, the only other Arab as far as she could tell in a twenty-strong crew of Spaniards. This had puzzled her enough to question it. But 'Expediency,' had been the only answer Rafiq would offer before it became another closed subject.

Since then she had eaten lunch with Rafiq and Faysal, and had been forced, because of Faysal's presence, to keep a lid on any other searching questions that might be burning in her head, which had been Rafiq's reason for including the other man, she was sure. And not once since he'd left her at the breakfast table had she laid eyes on Hassan—though she knew exactly where he was. Left alone to lie in the softer heat of the late afternoon, she was free to imagine him in what would be a custom built office, dealing with *matters of state*.

By phone, by fax, by internet—her mouth moved on a small smile. Hyped up, pumped up and doing what he loved to do most and in the interim forgetting the time and forgetting her! At other times she would have already been in there *reminding* him that there was a life other than *matters of state*. Closing her eyes, she could see his expression: the impatient glance at her interruption; the blank look that followed when she informed him of the time; the complaining sigh when she would insist on him stopping to share a cup of coffee or tea with her; and the way he would eventually surrender by reaching for her hand, then relaxing with a contented sigh…

In two stuffed chairs facing the window in his palace office—just like the two stuffed chairs strategically placed in the yacht's stateroom. Her heart gave a pinch; she tried to ignore what it was begging her to do.

*   *   *

Hassan was thinking along similar lines as he lay on the lounger next to hers. She was asleep. She didn't even know he was here. And not once in all the hours he had been locked away in his office had she come to interrupt.

Had he really expected her to? he asked himself. The answer that came back forced him to smother a hovering sigh because he didn't want to make a noise and waken her. They still had things to discuss, and the longer he put off the evil moment the better, as far as he was concerned, because he was going to get tough and she was not going to like it.

Another smothered sigh had him closing his eyes as he reflected back over the last few hours in which he had come as close as he had ever done to causing a split between the heads of the different families which together formed the Arabian state of Rahman.

Dynastic politics, he named it grimly. Al-Qadim and Al-Mukhtar against Al-Mahmud and Al-Yasin, with his right to decide for himself becoming lost in the tug of war. In the end he had been forced into a compromise that was no compromise at all—though he had since tried to turn it into one with the help of an old friend.

Leona released the sigh he had been struggling to suppress, and Hassan opened his eyes in time to see her yawn and stretch sinuously. Long and slender, sensationally curved yet exquisitely sleek. The colour of her hair, the smoothness of her lovely skin, the perfectly proportioned contours of her beautiful face. The eyes he could not see, the small straight nose that he could, the mouth he could feel against his mouth merely by looking at it. And—

Be done with it, he thought suddenly, and was on his feet and bending to scoop her into his arms.

She awoke with a start, saw it was him and sent him a sleepy frown. 'What are you doing?' she protested. 'I was comfortable there—'

'I know,' he replied. 'But I wish to be comfortable too, and I was not.'

He was already striding through the boat with a frown that

was far darker than hers. Across the foyer, up the three shallow steps. 'Open the door,' he commanded and was surprised when she reached down and did so without argument. He closed it with the help of a foot, saw her glance warily towards the bed. But it was to the two chairs that he took her, set her down in one of them, then lowered himself into the other with that sigh he had been holding back for so long.

'I suppose you have a good reason for moving me here,' she prompted after a moment.

'Yes,' he confirmed, and turned to look into those slumber darkened green eyes that tried so hard to hide her feelings from him but never ever quite managed to succeed. The wall of his chest contracted as he prepared himself for what he was about to say. 'You have been right all along.' He began with a confession. 'I am being pressured to take another wife…'

She should have expected it, Leona told herself as all hint of sleepy softness left her and her insides began to shake. She had always *known* it, so why was she feeling as if he had just reached out with a hand and strangled her heart? It was difficult to speak—almost impossible to speak—but she managed the burning question. 'Have you agreed?'

'No,' he firmly denied. 'Which is why you are here with me now—and more to the point, why you have to stay.'

Looking into his eyes, Leona could see that he was not looking forward to what he was going to say. She was right.

'A plot was conceived to have you abducted,' he told her huskily, 'the intention being to use your capture as a weapon with which to force my hand. When I discovered this I decided to foil their intentions by abducting you for myself.'

'Who?' she whispered, but had a horrible feeling she already knew the answer.

'Did the plotting? We are still trying to get that confirmed,' he said. 'But whoever it was they had their people watching your villa last night, waiting for Ethan and your father to leave for the party on the Petronades yacht. Once they had assured themselves that you were alone they meant to come in and take you.'

'Just like that,' she said shakily, and looked away from him as so many things began to fall into place. 'I felt their eyes on me,' she murmured. 'I knew they were there.'

'I suspected that you would do,' Hassan quietly commended. 'It is the kind of training we instilled into you that you never forget.'

'But this was different.' She got up, wrapped her arms around her body. 'I *knew* it felt different. I should have heeded that!'

'No—don't get upset.' Following suit, Hassan stood up and reached for her. She was as pale as a ghost and shaking like a leaf. 'My people were also there watching over you,' he assured. 'The car driver was my man, as was the man at the gate. I had people watching their people. There was not a single moment when you were not perfectly safe.'

'But to dislike me so much that they should *want* to take me!' Hurt beyond belief by that knowledge, Leona pushed him away, unwilling to accept his comfort. It had been hard enough to come to terms with it, when she'd believed he had snatched her back for his own purposes. But to discover now that he had done it because there was a plot against her was just too much to take. 'What is it with you people that you can't behave in a normal, rational manner?' she threw at him, eyes bright, hurt and accusing. 'You should have phoned *me* not my father!' she cried. 'You should have agreed to a divorce in the first place, then none of this would have happened at all!'

The *you people* sent Hassan's spine erect; the mention of divorce hardened his face. 'You are one of *my people*,' he reminded her curtly.

'No, I am not!' she denied with an angry shake of her head. 'I am just an ordinary person who had the misfortune to fall in love with the *extra*ordinary!'

'At least you are not going back to denying you love this

extraordinary person,' he noted arrogantly. 'And stop glaring at me like that!' he snapped. 'I am not your enemy!'

'Yes, you are!' Oh, why had she ever set eyes on this man? It would have been so much easier to have lived her life without ever having known him! 'So what happens now?' she demanded. 'Where do we go from here? Do I spend the rest of my days hiding from dark strangers just because you are too stubborn to let me go?'

'Of course not.' He was standing there frowning impatiently. 'Stop trying to build this into more than it actually is—'

More? 'Don't you think it is enough to know that I wasn't safe to be walking the streets in San Estéban? That my life and my basic human rights can be reduced to being worth nothing more than a mere pawn in some wretched person's power game?'

'I am sorry it has to come to this—'

Well, that just wasn't good enough! 'But you are no better yourself!' she threw at him angrily. 'Up to now you've used abduction, seduction and now you've moved onto intimidation to bring the wayward wife into line.' She listed. 'Should I be looking for the hidden cameras you are using so that you can show all of Rahman what a strong man you can be? Do I need to smile now?' she asked, watching his face grow darker with the sarcasm she tossed at him—and she just didn't care! 'Which way?' she goaded. 'Do I need to let Rafiq shroud me in an *abaya* again and even go as far as to abase myself at your exalted feet just to save your wretched face?'

'Say any more and you are likely to regret it,' he warned very grimly.

'I regret knowing you already!' Her eyes flashed, her body shook and her anger sparkled in the very air surrounding her. 'Next I suppose you will have me thrown into prison until I learn to behave myself!'

'This is it—' he responded, spreading his arms out wide in what was an outright provocation. 'Your prison. Now stop shouting at me like some undignified fishwife,' he snapped. 'We need to—'

'I want my life back without you in it!' Leona cut loudly across him.

What she got was the prince. The face, the eyes, his mood and his manner changed with the single blink of his long dark eyelashes. When his shoulders flexed it was like a dangerous animal slowly raising its hackles, and the fine hairs on her body suddenly became magnetised as she watched the metamorphosis take place. Her breathing snagged; her throat grew tight. He was standing perhaps three yards away from her but she could suddenly feel his presence as deeply as if he was a disturbing inch away.

'You want to live your life without me, then you may do so,' he announced. 'I will let you go, give you your divorce. There, it is done. *Inshallah*.' With a flick of the hand he strode across the room and calmly ordered tea!

It was retaliation at its most ruthless and it left her standing there utterly frozen with dismay. *Inshallah*. She couldn't even wince at what that single word represented. The will of Allah. Acceptance. A decision. The end. Hassan was agreeing to let her go and she could neither move nor breathe as the full power of that decree made its stunning impact.

She had not deserved that, Hassan was thinking impatiently as he stood glaring down at the telephone. She had been shocked, angry, hurt. Who would not be when they discovered that people they cared about, people they had tried to put before themselves, had been plotting to use them ruthlessly in a nasty game called politics? She had every right to vent her feelings—he had expected it! It was the reason why he had found them privacy before telling her the truth!

Or part of the truth, he then amended, all too grimly aware that there was yet more to come. But the rest was going to have to wait for a calmer time, for this moment might be silent but it certainly was not calm, because—

Damn it, despite the sensible lecture he was angry! There

was not another person on this planet who dared to speak to him as she had just done, and the hell if he was going to apologise for responding to that!

He flicked a glance at her. She hadn't moved. If she was even breathing he could see no evidence of it. Her hair was untidy. Long silken tendrils had escaped from the band she'd had it tied up in all day and were now caressing her nape, framing her stark white profile to add a vulnerability to her beauty that wrenched hard on his heart-strings. Her feet were bare, as were her slender arms and long slender legs. And she was emulating a statue again, only this time instead of art-deco she portrayed the discarded waif.

He liked the waif. His body quickened; another prohibited sigh tightened his chest. Curiosity replaced anger, though pride held his arrogant refusal to be the first one to retract his words firmly in place. She moved him like no other woman. She always had done. Angry or sad, hot with searing passion or frozen like ice as she was now.

Inshallah. It was Allah's will that he loved this woman above all others. Let her go? Not while he had enough breath in his body to fight to hold onto what was his! Though he wished he could see evidence that there was breath inside hers.

He picked up an ornament, measured the weight of the beautifully sculpted smooth sandstone camel then put it back down again to pick up another one of a falcon preparing to take off on the wing. And all the time the silence throbbed like a living pulse in the air all around them.

Say something—talk to me, he willed silently. Show me that my woman is still alive in there, he wanted to say. But that pride again was insisting he would not be the one to break the stunning deadlock they were now gripped in.

The light tap at the door meant the ordered tea he didn't even want had arrived. It was a relief to have something to do. She didn't move as he went to open the door, still hadn't moved when he closed it again on the steward he'd left firmly outside. Carrying the tray to the low table, he put it down, then turned to look at her. She still hadn't moved.

Inshallah, he thought again, and gave up the battle. Walking over to her, he placed a hand against her pale cheek, stroked his thumb along the length of her smooth throat then settled it beneath her chin so he could lift her face up that small inch it required to make her look at him.

Eyes of a lush dark vulnerable green gazed into sombre night-dark brown. Her soft mouth parted; at last she took a breath he could hear and see. 'Be careful what you wish for,' she whispered helplessly.

His legs went hollow. He understood. It was the way it had always been with them. 'If true love could be made to order, we would still be standing here,' he told her gravely.

At which point the ice melted, the gates opened and in a single painfully hopeless move she coiled her arms around his neck, buried her face into his chest and began to weep.

So what do you do with a woman who breaks her heart for you? You take her to bed. You wrap her in yourself. You make love to her until it is the only thing that matters any more. Afterwards, you face reality again. Afterwards you pick up from where you should never have let things go astray.

The tea stewed in the pot. Evening settled slowly over the room with a display of sunset colours that changed with each deepening stage of their sensual journey. Afterwards, he carried her into the shower and kept reality at bay by loving her there. Then they washed each other, dried each other, touched and kissed and spoke no words that could risk intrusion for as long as they possibly could.

It was Leona who eventually approached reality. 'What now?' she asked him.

'We sail the ocean on our self-made island, and keep the rest of the world out,' he answered huskily.

'For how long?'

'As long as we possibly can.' He didn't have the heart to

tell her he knew exactly how long. The rest would wait, he told himself.

It was a huge tactical error, though he did not know that yet. For he had not retracted what he had decreed in a moment of anger. And, although Leona might appear to have set the words aside, she had not forgotten them. Nor had she forgotten the reason she was here at all: there were people out there who wanted to harm her.

But for now they pretended that everything was wonderful. Like a second honeymoon in fact—if an unusual one with Rafiq and Faysal along for company. They laughed a lot and played like any other set of holidaymakers would. Matters of state took a back seat to other more pleasurable pursuits. They windsurfed off the Greek islands, snorkelled over shipwrecks, jet-skied in parts of the Mediterranean that were so empty of other human life that they could have had the sea to themselves.

One week slid stealthily into a second week Leona regained the weight she had lost during the empty months without Hassan, and her skin took on a healthy golden hue. When matters of state refused to be completely ignored, Rafiq was always on hand to help keep up the pretence that everything was suddenly and miraculously okay.

Then it came. One heat-misted afternoon when Hassan was locked away in his office, and Faysal, Leona and Rafiq were lazing on the shade deck sipping tall cool drinks and reading a book each. She happened to glance up and received the shock of her life when she saw that they were sailing so close to land it felt as if she could almost reach out and touch it.

'Oh, good grief,' Getting up she went to stand by the rail. 'Where are we, Rafiq?'

'At the end of our time here alone together,' a very different voice replied.

CHAPTER SIX

LEONA turned to find Hassan was standing not far away and Rafiq was in the process of rising to his feet. One man was looking at her; the other one was making sure that he didn't. Hassan's words shimmered in the air separating them and Rafiq's murmured, 'Excuse me, I will leave you to it,' was as revealing as the speed with which he left.

The silence that followed his departure pulsed with the flurried pace of her heartbeat while Leona waited for Hassan to clarify what he had just said.

He was still in the same casual shorts and shirt he had been wearing when she had last seen him, she noticed. But there, the similarity between this man and the man who had kissed the top of her head and strolled away to answer Faysal's call to work a short hour ago ended. For there was a tension about him that was almost palpable, and in his hand he held a gold fountain pen which offered up an image of him getting up from his desk to come back here at such speed that he hadn't even had time to drop the pen.

'We arrived here sooner than I had anticipated,' he said, confirming her last thought.

'It would be helpful for me to know where *here* is,' she replied in a voice laden with the weight of whatever it was that was about to come at her.

And come it did. 'Port Said,' he provided, saw her startled response of recognition and lowered his eyes on an acknowledging grimace that more or less said the rest.

Port Said lay at the mouth of the Suez Canal, which linked the Mediterranean with the Red Sea. If they were coming into the port, then there could only be one reason for it:

Hassan was ready to go home and their self-made, sea-borne paradise was about to disintegrate.

He had noticed the pen in his hand and went to drop it on the lounger next to the book she had left there. Then he walked over to the long white table at which they had eaten most of their evening meals over the last two weeks. Pulling out a chair, he sat down, released a sigh, then put up a hand to rub the back of his neck as if he was trying to iron out a crick.

When he removed it again he stretched the hand out towards her. 'Join me,' he invited.

Leona shook her head and instead found her arms crossing tightly beneath the thrust of her breasts. 'Tell me first,' she insisted.

'Don't be difficult,' he censured. 'I want you here, within touching distance when I explain.'

But she didn't want to be within touching distance when he said what she knew he had to say. 'You are about to go home, aren't you?'

'Yes,' he confirmed.

It was all right challenging someone to tell you the truth when you did not mind the answer, but when you did mind it— 'So this is it,' she stated, finding a short laugh from somewhere that was not really a laugh at all. 'Holiday over...'

Out there the sun glistened on the blue water, casting a shimmering haze over the nearing land. It was hot but she was cold. It was bright but she was standing in darkness. The end, she thought. The finish.

'So, how are you going to play it?' she asked him. 'Do you drop me off on the quay in the clothes I arrived in and wave a poignant farewell as you sail away. Or have I earned my passage back to San Estéban?'

'What are you talking about?' Hassan frowned. 'You are my wife, yet you speak about yourself as a mistress.'

Which was basically how she had been behaving over the

last two weeks, Leona admitted to herself. '*Inshallah*,' she murmured.

The small sarcasm brought him back to his feet. As he strode towards her she felt her body quicken, felt her breasts grow tight and despised herself for being so weak of the flesh that she could be aroused by a man who was about to carry out his promise to free her. But six feet two inches of pedigree male to her five feet seven was such a lot to ignore when she added physical power into the equation, then included mental power and sexual power. It really was no wonder she was such a weakling where he was concerned.

And it didn't stop there, because he came to brace his hands on the rail either side of her, then pushed his dark face close up to hers. Now she could feel the heat of him, feel his scented breath on her face. She even responded to the ever-present sexual glow in his eyes though it had no right to be there—in either of them.

'A mistress knows when to keep her beautiful mouth shut and just listen. A wife does her husband the honour of hearing him out before she makes wildly inaccurate claims,' he said.

'You've just told me that our time here is over,' she reminded him with a small tense shrug of one slender shoulder. 'What else is there left for you to say?'

'What I said,' he corrected, 'was that our time here *alone* was over.'

The difference made her frown. Hassan used the moment to shift his stance, grasp both of her hands and pry them away from the death grip they had on her arms. Her fingers left marks where they had been clinging. He frowned at the marks and sighed at her pathetically defiant face. Then, dropping one of her hands, he turned and pulled her over to the table, urged her down into the chair he had just vacated and, still without letting go of her other hand, pulled out a second chair upon which he sat down himself.

He drew the chair so close to her own that he had to spread his thighs wide enough to enclose hers. It was a very effective way to trap his audience, especially when he leaned forward and said, 'Now, listen, because this is important and I will not have you diverting me by tossing up insignificant comments.'

It was automatic that she should open her mouth to question that remark. It was predictable, she supposed, that Hassan should stop her by placing his free hand across her parted lips. 'Shh,' he commanded, 'for I refuse to be distracted yet again because the anguish shows in your eyes each time we reach this moment, and your words are only weapons you use to try and hide that from me.'

'Omniscient' was the word that came to mind to describe him, she thought, as her eyes told him she would be quiet. His hand slid away from her face, leaving its warm imprint on her skin. He smiled a brief smile at her acquiescence, then went so very serious that she found herself holding onto her breath.

'You know,' he began, 'that above all things my father has always been your strongest ally, and it is for him that I am about to speak…'

The moment he mentioned Sheikh Khalifa her expressive eyes clouded with concern.

'As his health fails, the more he worries about the future of Rahman,' he explained. 'He frets about everything. You, me, what I will do if the pressures currently being brought to bear upon me force me to make a decision which could change the rule of Rahman.'

'You mean you have actually considered giving up your right to succession?' Leona gasped out in surprise.

'It is an option,' he confessed. 'And one which became more appealing after I uncovered the plot involving you, which was aimed to make me do as other people wish,' he added cynically. 'But for my father's sake I assured him that I am not about to walk away from my duty. So he decided to fret about my happiness if I am forced to sacrifice you for the sake of harmony, which places me in a frustrating no-win situation where his peace of mind is concerned.'

'I'm sorry,' she murmured.

'I don't want your sympathy, I want your help,' he stated with a shortness that told her how much he disliked having to ask. 'He loves you, Leona, you know that. He has missed you badly since you left Rahman.'

'I didn't completely desert him, Hassan.' She felt pushed into defending herself. 'I've spoken to him every day via the internet.' Even here on the yacht she had been using Faysal's computer each morning to access her e-mail. 'I even read the same books he is reading so that we can discuss them together. I—'

'I know,' Hassan cut in with a wry smile. 'What you say to him he relays to me, so I am fully aware that I am a bully and a tyrant, a man without principle and most definitely my father's son.'

'I said those things to tease a laugh out of him,' she defended.

'I know this too,' he assured her. 'But he likes to make me smile with him.' Reaching up, he stroked a finger along the flush of discomfort that had mounted her cheeks. 'And let me face it,' he added, removing the finger, 'your communication with him was far sweeter than your communication with me.'

He was referring to the letters he'd received from her lawyer. 'It was over between us. You should have left it like that.'

'It is not over between us, and I *cannot* leave it like that.'

'Your father—'

'Needs you,' he grimly inserted. '*I* need you to help me ease his most pressing concerns. So I am asking you for a full and open reconciliation of our marriage—for my father's sake if not for yours and mine.'

Leona wasn't a fool. She knew what he was *not* saying here. 'For how long?'

He offered a shrug. 'How long is a piece of string?' he posed whimsically. Then, because he could see that the answer was not enough, he dropped the whimsy, sat right back in his seat and told her curtly, 'The doctors give him two months—three at most. In that period we have been warned to expect a rapid deterioration as the end draws near. So I ask you to do this one thing for him and help to make his passage out of this world a gentle one…'

Oh, dear heaven, she thought, putting a hand up to her eyes as the full weight of what he was asking settled over her. How could she refuse? She didn't even want to refuse. She loved that old man as much as she loved her own father. But there were other issues here which had not been aired yet, and it was those that kept her agreement locked inside.

'The other wife they want for you,' she prompted, 'am I to appear to accept her imminent arrival also?'

His expression darkened. 'Do me the honour of allowing me some sensitivity,' he came back. 'I have no wish to sacrifice your face for my own face. And I find it offensive that you could suspect that I would do.'

Which was very fine and noble of him but— 'She is still there, hovering in the shadows, Hassan,' Leona said heavily. She could even put a name to the woman, though he probably didn't know that she could. 'And taking me back to Rahman does not solve your problems with the other family leaders unless you take that other wife.'

'The old ones and I have come to an agreement,' he informed her. 'In respect for my father, they will let the matter ride while he is still alive.'

'Then what?'

'I will deal with them when I have to, but for the next few months anyway, my father's peace of mind must come first.'

And so, he was therefore saying, should it for her. 'Will you do this?'

The outright challenge. 'Did you really think that I would not?' She sighed, standing up and pushing her chair away so that she could step around him.

'You're angry.' His eyes narrowed on her sparkling eyes and set expression.

Anger didn't nearly cover what she was really feeling. 'In principle I agree to play the doting wife again,' she said. 'But in fact I am now going to go away and *sulk* as you like to call it. Because no matter how well you wrap it all up in words of concern, Hassan, you are as guilty for using me in much the same way my foiled abductors intended to use me, and that makes you no better than them, does it?'

With that she turned and walked away, and Hassan allowed her to, because he knew she was speaking the truth so had nothing he could offer in his own defence.

Within seconds Rafiq appeared with a question written into the hard lines of his face.

'Don't ask,' he advised heavily. 'And she does not even know the half of it yet.'

'Which half does she not know,' Rafiq asked anyway.

'What comes next,' Hassan replied, watching his half-brother's eyes slide over his left shoulder. He spun to see what he was looking at, then began cursing when he saw how close they were to reaching their reserved berth in Port Said. 'How long?' he demanded.

'You have approximately one hour before the first guests begin to arrive.'

A small hour to talk, to soothe, to plead yet again for more charity from a woman who had given enough as it was. 'You had better prepare yourself to take my place, Rafiq,' he gritted. 'Because, at this precise moment, I am seriously considering jumping ship with my wife and forgetting I possess a single drop of Al-Qadim blood.'

'Our father may not appreciate such a decision,' Rafiq commented dryly.

'That reminder,' Hassan turned to snap, 'was not necessary.'

'I was merely covering for myself,' his half brother defended. 'For I have no wish to walk in your shoes, my lord Sheikh.'

About to go after Leona, Hassan paused. 'What do you wish for?' he questioned curiously.

'Ah.' Rafiq sighed. 'At this precise moment I wish for midnight, when I should be with *my* woman in a hotel room in Port Said. For tonight she flies in to dance for visiting royalty by special request. But later she will dance only for me and I will worship at her feet. Then I will worship other parts of her until dawn, after which I will reluctantly return here, to your exalted service, my lord sheikh,' he concluded with a mocking bow.

Despite the weight of his mood, Hassan could not resist a smile. 'You should change your plans and bring her to dinner,' he suggested. 'The sheer sensation she would cause would be a diversion I would truly appreciate.'

'But would Leona?' Rafiq pondered.

Instantly all humour died from Hassan's face. 'Leona,' he predicted. 'is in no frame of mind to appreciate anything.'

And on that grim reminder, he went off to find *his* woman, while half wishing that he was the one treading in Rafiq's shoes.

He found her without difficulty, shut behind the bathroom door and hiding in the steam being produced by the shower. The fact that she had not bothered to lock the door spoke volumes as to her mood. Hassan could visualise the angry way she would have walked in here, throwing the door shut behind her then taking the rest of her anger out on the heap of clothes he could see tossed onto the floor.

So what did he do now? Go back to the bedroom and wait for her to reappear, or did he throw caution to the wind, strip off and just brave her fiery den?

It was not really a question since he was already taking off his clothes. For this was no time to be feeble. Leona had agreed *in principle*, so now she was about to learn the consequences of that. With a firming of his mouth he opened the shower-cubicle door, stepped inside and closed it again.

She was standing just out of reach of the shower jets with her head tipped back as she massaged shampoo into her hair. Streams of foaming bubbles were sliding over wet gold skin, collecting around the tips of her tilted breasts and snaking through the delightful valley in between to pool in the perfect oval of her navel, before spilling out to continue their way towards the chestnut cluster marking the apex with her slender thighs.

His body awoke; he allowed himself a rueful smile at how little it took to make him want this beautiful creature. Then she realised he was there and opened her eyes, risking soap burn so that she could kill him with a look.

'What do you want now?' she demanded.

Since the answer to that question was indubitably obvious, he didn't bother with a reply. Instead he reached for the container of foaming body soap, pumped a generous amount into the palm of his hand and began applying it to her skin. Her hands dropped from her hair and pressed hard against his chest in an effort to push him away.

'Thank you,' he said, and calmly pumped some soap onto his own chest as if it was a foregone conclusion that she would wash him. 'Sharing can turn the simplest of chores into the best of pleasures, do you not think?'

The green light in her eyes took on a distinctly threatening gleam. 'I think you're arrogant and hateful and I want you to get out of here,' she coldly informed him.

'Close your eyes,' he advised. 'The shampoo is about to reach them.'

Then, even as she lifted a hand to swipe the bubbles away, he reached up and directed the shower head at her so that the steamy spray hit her full in the face. While gasping at the shock, he made his next move, turned the spray away and replaced it with his mouth.

For a sweet, single moment he allowed himself to believe he'd made the easy conquest. It usually worked. On any other occasion it would have worked as a tasty starter to other ways of forgetfulness. But this time he received a sharp dig in the ribs for his optimism, and a set of teeth closed threateningly on his bottom lip until he eased the pressure and lifted his head. Her eyes spat fire and brimstone at him.

He arched an eyebrow and glided a defiant hand down to the silken warmth of her abdomen.

'You are treading on dangerous ground, Sheikh,' she warned him.

'I am?'

She ignored the message in his tone. 'I have nothing I want to say to you. So why don't you leave me alone?'

'But I was not offering to talk,' he explained, and boldly slid the hand lower.

'You are not doing *that* either!' Squirming away like a slippery snake, she ended up pressed against the corner of the cubicle, eyes like green lasers trying their best to obliterate him. One arm was covering her breasts, the other hand was protecting other parts. She looked like some sweet, cowering virgin, but he was not fooled by the vision. This beautiful wife of his possessed a temper that could erupt without warning. At the moment it was merely simmering.

'Okay.' With an ease that threw her into frowning confusion, he conceded the battle to her, pumped more soap onto his chest and began to wash while trying to ignore the obvious fact that a certain part of him was as hard as a rock and begging he do something about it. 'We did not really have time, anyway. Our guests arrive in less than an hour...'

'Guests?' she looked up sharply. 'What guests?'

'The guests we are about to transport to Rahman to attend the anniversary of my father's thirtieth year of rule, which will take place in ten days' time,' he replied while calmly sluicing the soap from his body as if he had not dropped yet another bomb at her feet. 'Here.' He frowned. 'Wash the shampoo from your hair before you really do hurt your eyes.' And he stepped back to allow her access to the spray.

Leona didn't move; she didn't even notice that he had. She was too busy suffering from one shock too many. 'How long have you known you were taking on guests?'

'A while.' Reaching up to unhook the shower head from the wall, he then pulled her towards him to began rinsing the shampoo from her hair for himself.

'But you didn't feel fit to tell me before now?'

'I did not feel fit to do anything but enjoy being with you.' Pushing up her chin, he sent the slick, clean pelt of her hair sliding down her spine with the help of the shower jet. 'Why?' He asked a question of his own. 'Would knowing have had any bearing on your decision to come back to Rahman with me?'

Would it? Leona asked herself, when really she did not need to, because she knew her answer would have been the same. He was rinsing the rest of her now and she just stood there and let him do it. Only a few minutes ago his smallest touch had infused her with that need to feel him deep inside her, now she could not remember what the need felt like. As she waited for him to finish administering to her wooden form, she noticed that his passion had died too.

'I suppose I had better know if there is anything else you haven't bothered to tell me,' she murmured eventually.

His pause before speaking could have been a hesitation over his answer, or it could have been a simple pause while he switched off the shower. 'Just the names of our guests,' he said. 'And that can wait until we have dealt with the more urgent task of drying ourselves and getting dressed.'

With that he opened the shower door and stepped out to collect a towel, which he folded around her before offering her another one for her hair. For himself he reached for a towelling bathrobe, pulled it on and headed for the door.

'Hassan…' she made him pause '…the rest of this trip and your father's celebration party—am I being put on public show for a specific purpose?'

'Some people need to be shown that I will not be coerced in any way,' he answered without turning. 'And my father wants you there. This will be his last anniversary. I will deny him nothing.'

At Hassan's request, she was wearing a calf-length white silk tunic studded with pearl-white sequins that shimmered when she moved. In accordance with Arabian tradition, the tunic had a high neckline, long sleeves and a pair of matching slender silk trousers that covered her legs. On her head she had draped a length of fine silk, and beneath it her hair had been carefully pleated into a glossy, smooth coronet. Her make-up was so understated you could barely tell it was there except for the flick of black mascara highlighting the length of her eyelashes and the hint of a gloss to her soft pink mouth.

Beside her stood the Prince. Dressed in a white silk tunic and gold silk top robe, on his head he wore a white *gutrah* ringed by three circles of gold. To her other side and one short pace behind stood Rafiq, dressed almost exactly the same as his brother only without the bands of gold. And as they waited in the boat's foyer, Leona was in no doubt that the way they were presented was aimed to make a specific statement.

Sheikh Hassan ben Khalifa Al-Qadim and his wife the Sheikha Leona Al-Qadim—bestowed upon her at her request, for the woman of Arabia traditionally kept their father's name—were ready to formally receive guests, whether those guests were friends or foes.

Rafiq was their guardian, their protector, their most respected brother and trusted friend. He possessed his own title, though he had never been known to use it. He possessed the right to wear the gold bands of high office, but no one had ever seen them circling his head. His power rode on the back of his indifference to anything that did not interest him. His threat lay in the famed knowledge that he would lay down his life for these two people standing in front of him, plus the father he loved without question.

His presence here, therefore, made its own loud statement; come in friendship and be at peace; come in conflict and beware.

Why? Because the first person to tread the gangway onto the yacht was Sheikh Abdul Al-Yasin and his wife, Zafina. Hassan and Rafiq knew that Sheikh Abdul was behind the plot to abduct Leona, but the sheikh did not know the brothers knew. Which was why he felt safe in taking the bait handed out for this trip—namely a meeting of the chiefs during a cruise on the Red Sea, in which his aim was to beat Hassan into submission about this second wife he was being so stubborn in refusing.

What none of them knew was that Leona suspected it was Sheikh Abdul who had planned her abduction. Because she knew about Nadira, his beautiful daughter, who had been held up to her many times as the one chosen to take that coveted place in Sheikh Hassan's life as his second wife.

'Ah—Hassan!' The two men greeted and shook hands pleasantly enough. 'You will be pleased to know that I left your father in better sorts than of late. I saw him this morning before I caught my flight to Cairo.'

'I must thank you for keeping him company while we have been away,' Hassan replied.

'No thanks—no thanks.' Sheikh Abdul refused them. 'It was my privilege—Leona…' He turned towards her next, though offered no physical contact as was the Arab way. He bowed instead. 'You have been away too long. It is good to see you here.'

'Thank you.' She found a smile, wished she dared search for the comfort of Hassan's hand, but such shows of weakness would be pounced upon and dissected when she was not there to hear it happen.

'Rafiq.' His nodded greeting was distinctly wary. 'You made a killing with your stock in Schuler-Kleef, I see.'

'My advice is usually sound, sir,' Rafiq replied respectfully. 'I take it you did not buy some for yourself?'

'I forgot.'

Through all of this, Sheikh Abdul's wife, Zafina, stood back in total silence, neither stepping forward to follow the line of introduction nor attempting to remind her husband of her presence. It was such a quiescent stance, one that Leona had grown used to from the women of Rahman when they were out in the company of their men.

But it was a quiescence that usually only lasted as long as it took them to be alone with the other women. Then the real

personalities shot out to take you by surprise. Some were
soft and kind, some cold and remote, some alive with fun.
Zafina was a woman who knew how to wield her power from
within the female ranks and had no hesitation in doing so if
it furthered her own particular cause. It was due to her clever
machinations that her son had married another sheikh's most
favoured daughter.

She'd had Hassan marked for her daughter, Nadira, from
the day the child had been born. Therefore, in her eyes, she
had every reason to dislike Leona. And, tranquil though she
might appear right now, Leona could feel resentment flowing
towards her in waves.

'Zafina.' She stepped forward, deciding to take the polite
stand. 'You are well, I trust? Thank you for taking time out
of your busy life to join us here.'

'The pleasure is all mine, Sheikha,' the older woman replied. But then her husband was listening and so was the
coveted Sheikh Hassan. 'You have lost weight, I think. But
Sheikh Khalifa tells me you have been sick?'

Someone had told her at any rate, but Leona suspected it
was not Hassan's father. Thankfully other guests began to
arrive. Sheikh Jibril Al-Mahmud and his timid wife, Medina,
who looked to her husband before she dared so much as
breathe.

Sheikh Imran Al-Mukhtar and his youngest son, Samir,
arrived next. Like a light at the end of a tunnel, Samir put
the first genuine smile on everyone's face because he broke
right through every stiff convention being performed in the
yacht's foyer, and headed directly for Leona. 'My princess!'
he greeted, picked her up in his arms then swung her around.

'Put her down,' his father censured. 'Rafiq has that glint
in his eye.'

'Not Hassan?' Samir questioned quizzically.

'Hassan knows what belongs to him, Rafiq is merely over-
protective. And everyone else simply disapproves of your
loose ways.'

And there it was, tied up in one neat comment, Hassan

noted as he watched Leona laugh down into Samir's handsome young face. Al-Qadim and Al-Mukhtar set apart from Al-Mahmud and Al-Yasin. It promised to be an interesting trip. For the first time in two weeks they used the formal dining room on the deck above. White-liveried stewards served them through many courses, and the conversation around the table was pleasant and light, mainly due to Samir, who refused to allow the other men to sink into serious discussion, and even the other women unbent beneath his boyish charm.

But Leona was quiet. From his end of the table Hassan watched her speak when spoken to, smiling in all the right places. He watched her play the perfect hostess in that easy, unassuming way he remembered well, where everyone's needs were predicted and met before they knew they were missing something. But occasionally, when she thought no one was attending her, he watched the corners of her mouth droop with short releases of the tension she was experiencing.

Sad. Her eyes were sad. He had hurt her with his drippingtap method of feeding information to her. Now here she sat, having to pretend everything was perfect between them, when really she wanted to kill him for waiting until the last minute to spring all of this.

His heart clenched when he caught sight of her impulsive grin as she teasingly cuffed Samir for saying something outrageous. She had not laughed with him like that since the first night they'd been together again. No matter how much she had smiled, played, teased—loved him—during the last two weeks, he had been aware of an inner reserve that told him he no longer had all of her. Her spirit was missing, he named it grimly. It had been locked away out of his reach.

I love you, he wanted to tell her. But loving did not mean much to a woman who felt that she was trapped between a rock and a hard place.

A silence suddenly reigned. It woke him up from his own thoughts to notice that Leona was staring down at the plate in front of her and Samir had frozen in dismay. What had he missed? What had been said? Muscles began tightening all over him. Rafiq was looking at him for guidance. His skin began to crawl with the horrible knowledge that he had just missed something supremely important, and he could not think of a single thing to say!

His half-brother took the initiative by coming to his feet. 'Leona, you will understand if I beg to leave you now,' he petitioned as smooth as silk, while Hassan, who knew him better than anyone, could see him almost pulsing with rage.

Leona's head came up as, with a flickering blink of her lashes, she made the mammoth effort to pull herself together. 'Oh, yes, of course, Rafiq,' she replied, having absolutely no idea, Hassan was sure, why Rafiq was excusing himself halfway through dinner, and at this precise moment she didn't care. It was a diversion. She needed the diversion. It should have been himself who provided it.

'I need a word before you leave,' he said to Rafiq, and got to his feet. 'Samir, do the honours and replenish my wife's glass with wine.'

The poor young man almost leapt at the wine bottle, relieved to have something to do. As Rafiq walked past Hassan, with a face like fury, Hassan saw Leona reach out and gently touch Samir's hand, as if to assure him that everything was all right.

'What did I miss in there?' he rapped out at Rafiq as soon as they were out of earshot.

'If I did not like Samir I would strangle him,' Rafiq responded harshly. 'Leona asked him how his mother was. He went into a long and humorous story about her sitting in wait for his sister to give birth. Leona dealt with that. She even laughed in all the right places. But then the fool had to suggest it was time that she produced your son and heir.'

'He cannot have known what he was saying,' Hassan said angrily.

'It was not the question which threw Leona, it was the resounding silence that followed it and the bleak expression upon your face! Where were you, man?' Rafiq wanted to know. It was so rare that he used that tone with Hassan, that the censure in it carried twice the weight.

'My mind had drifted for a few seconds,' he answered tensely.

'And the expression?'

'Part of the drift,' he admitted heavily.

'You were supposed to be on the alert at all times for attacks of this kind.' Rafiq was not impressed. 'It was risk enough to bring onto this boat the man who wishes her ill, without you allowing your mind to drift.'

'Stop spitting words at my neck and go to your dancer,' Hassan snapped back impatiently. 'You know as well as I do that neither Abdul or Jibril would dare to try anything when they are here for the specific purpose of talking me round!'

It's okay, Leona was telling herself. I can deal with it. I've always known that deep inside he cared more than he ever let me see. So, he had been caught by surprise and showed the truth to everyone. *I* was caught by surprise and showed it myself.

'Samir,' she murmured gently. 'If you pour me any more wine I will be sozzled and fall over when I have to stand up.'

'Hassan wants your glass kept full.' He grimly kept on pouring.

'Hassan was attempting to fill an empty gap in the conversation, not put me under the table,' she dryly pointed out.

Samir sat back with a sigh. 'I want to die a thousands deaths,' he heavily confessed.

Hassan arrived back at the table. Leona felt his glance sear a pointed message at her down the table's length. She refused to catch his eye, and smiled and smiled until her jaw ached.

After that, the rest of the dinner passed off without further incident. But by the time the ladies left the men alone and removed to the adjoining salon Leona was in no mood for a knife-stabbing session. So she was actually relieved that Medina and Zafina chose to stab at her indirectly by discussing Zafina's daughter, Nadira, whose beauty, it seemed, had multiplied during the last year. And as for her grace and quiet gentle ways—she was going to make some lucky man the perfect wife one day.

At least they didn't prose on about how wonderful she was with children, Leona thought dryly, as the conversation was halted when Hassan brought the men through within minutes of the ladies leaving them.

The evening dragged on. She thought about the other days and nights still to come and wondered if she was going to get through them all in one piece. Eventually the other two women decided they were ready to retire. A maid was called and within minutes of them leaving Leona was happy to follow suit. As she stepped outside, Hassan joined her. It was the first time he had managed to get her alone since the incident at the dinner table.

'I am at your feet,' he murmured contritely. 'I was miles away and had no idea what had taken place until Rafiq explained it to me.'

She didn't believe him, but it was nice of him to try the cover-up, she supposed. 'Samir wins hands down on apologies,' she came back. 'He wants to die a thousands deaths.'

With that she walked away, shaking inside and not really sure why she was. She got ready for bed and crawled between the cool cotton sheets, sighed, punched the pillow, then attempted to fall asleep. She must have managed it, because the next thing she knew a warm body was curling itself in behind her.

'I don't recall our new deal involving having to share a bed,' she said coldly.

'I don't recall offering to sleep elsewhere,' Hassan coolly returned. 'So go back to sleep.' The arm he folded around her aimed to trap. 'And, since I am as exhausted as you are, you did not need the silk pyjamas to keep my lecherous desires at bay…'

'I really hate you sometimes.' She wanted the last word.

'Whereas I will love you with my dying breath. And when they lay us in our final resting place in our crypt of gold it will be like this, with the scent of your beautiful hair against my face and my hand covering your lying little heart. There,' he concluded, 'is that flowery enough to beat Samir's one thousand deaths?'

Despite not wanting to, she giggled. It was her biggest mistake. The exhausted man became an invigorated man. His lecherous desires took precedence.

Did she try to stop him? No, she did not. Did she even want to? No, again. Did he know all of that before he started removing the pyjamas?' Of course he did. And there was something needle-piercingly poignant in this man losing touch with everything but this kind of loving as he came inside her, cupped her face with his hands and held her gaze with his own, as he drove them towards that other resting place.

CHAPTER SEVEN

MORNING came too soon, to Leona's regret. Although here, shut inside this room and wrapped in the relative sanctuary of Hassan's arms, she could let herself pretend for a little while longer that everything was perfect.

He was perfect, she observed tenderly as she studied the lean smooth lines of his dark golden face. He slept quietly—he always had done—lips parted slightly, black lashes lying still against the silken line of his cheekbones. Her heart began to squeeze and her stomach muscles joined in. This deep-rooted attraction he had always inspired in her had never diminished no matter what else had come in between.

She released a sigh that feathered his face and made his nose twitch. And it was such a nose, she thought with a smile, irresistibly reaching up to run a fingertip down its long silken length.

'Life can have its perfect moments,' a sleepy voice drawled.

Since she had been thinking much the same herself, Leona moved that bit closer so she could brush a kiss on his mouth.

Eyelashes drifted upward, revealing ebony irises packed with love. 'Does the kiss mean you have forgiven me for dropping all of this on you?'

'Shh,' she whispered, 'or you will spoil it.'

'Kiss me again, then,' he insisted. So she did. Why not? she asked herself. This was her man. Rightly or wrongly he was most definitely hers here and now.

It was a shame the ring of the telephone beside the bed had to intrude, or one thing would have led to another before they should have needed to face reality again. As it was, Hassan released a sigh and reached out to hook up the receiver. A few seconds later he was replacing it again and reaching out to touch her kiss-warmed mouth with a look of regret.

'Duty calls,' he murmured.

Ah, duty, Leona thought, and flopped heavily onto her back. Perfect moment over, pretence all gone. Stripped clean to his smooth dark golden skin, it was the prince who rose up from the bed and without saying another word disappeared into the bathroom.

He came out again ten minutes later, wrapped in fluffy white cotton and looking as handsome as sin. Wishing his pull wasn't as strong on her senses, she got up with a definite reluctance to face the day mirrored on her face, pulled on her wrap and went to take her turn in the bathroom.

But Hassan stopped her as she walked past him, his hand gently cupping her chin. He smelt of soap and minted toothpaste as he bent to kiss her cheek. 'Fifteen minutes, on the sun deck,' he instructed as he straightened again. 'For breakfast with an added surprise.'

The 'added surprise' made Leona frown. 'You promised me you had no more surprises waiting to jump out at me,' she protested.

'But this one does not count,' he said with a distinctly worrying gleam in his eye. 'So hurry up, wear something deliciously stylish that will wow everyone, and prepare yourself to fall on my neck.'

'Fall on his neck,' Leona muttered to herself as she showered. She had developed a distinct aversion to surprises since arriving on this wretched boat so she was more likely to strangle him.

In a pale blue sundress made of a cool cotton, and with her red hair floating loose about her shoulders—because she felt like wearing it as a banner, which made a statement about…something, though she wasn't absolutely sure what—Leona walked out onto the sun deck to find Rafiq there but no Hassan.

He looked up, smiled, then stood to pull out a chair for

her. He was back in what she called his off-duty clothes, loose-fitting black chinos and a white V-neck tee shirt that did things to his muscled shape no one saw when he was covered in Arab robes.

'Was your mother an Amazon, by any chance?' she enquired caustically, because his father was a fine boned little man and Rafiq had to have got his size from someone.

The waspishness in her tone earned her a sharp glance. 'Did you climb out of bed on the wrong side, by any chance?' he threw back.

'I *hate* surprises,' she announced as she sat down.

'Ah,' Rafiq murmured. 'So you have decided to take it out on me because I am unlikely to retaliate.'

He was right, and she knew it, which didn't help this terrible, restless tension she was suffering from. 'Where is Hassan?' She strove for a nicer tone and managed to half succeed. 'He said he would be here.'

'The pilot who will guide us through the Suez Canal has arrived,' Rafiq explained. 'It is an expected courtesy for Hassan to greet him personally.'

Glancing outwards, Leona saw Port Said sprawling out in front of them like a vast industrial estate. It was not the prettiest of views to have with your breakfast, even though they seemed to have got the best of the berths, moored way off to one side in a separate harbour that looked as if it was reserved for the luxury private crafts.

'And the rest of our guests?' she enquired next, aware that she probably should have asked about them first.

'Either still asleep or breakfasting in their suites.'

Mentioning sleep had a knock-on effect on him, and in the next moment Rafiq was stifling a yawn. It was only then that Leona recalled his slick retreat from the fray the evening before.

'Up all night?' The spike was back in her voice.

He didn't reply, but the rueful way his mouth tilted suddenly made her think of Spanish dancers. 'I hope she was good.' She took a tart stab in the dark.

'Delightful.' He smiled. It was yet another blow to her fragile ego that her one solid ally had deserted her last night for another woman. 'Here,' he said gently, and began to pour her out a cup of tea. 'Maybe this will help soothe your acid little tongue.'

Something needed to, Leona silently admitted as she picked up the cup. She had never felt so uptight and anxious, and it all was down to Hassan and surprises she did not want and people she did not want to be with and a marriage she did not—

The slightly sweet scent of Earl Grey suddenly turned her stomach. She must have gone pale because Rafiq began frowning. 'What is the matter?' he demanded.

'I think the milk must be off,' she explained, hastily putting the cup back on its saucer then pushing it away.

The sickly sensation left her almost as suddenly as it had hit. Problem solved in her mind, she wasn't convinced when Rafiq picked up the jug to sniff at the milk and announced, 'It seems fine to me.'

But he rose anyway and went to replace the milk with fresh from the cartons kept in the refrigerator situated just inside the salon. Then Hassan appeared and the incident was forgotten because, after dropping a kiss on her forehead, he went to pull out the chair next to Rafiq, who was just returning to the table with the fresh jug of milk. For a moment Leona was held captivated by how much alike the two men were. Even their clothes were similar, only Hassan wore beige chinos and a black tee shirt.

Men of beauty no matter what clothes they were wore, she mused a trifle breathlessly, knowing that she would be hard put to it to find two more perfect specimens. So why do I love them both so differently? she asked herself as she watched them sit down. Life would certainly have been a whole lot simpler if she'd fallen in love with Rafiq instead of Hassan. No strict calls to duty, no sheikhdom to rule, no onus to produce the next son and heir to his vast power and untold fortune.

But she loved Rafiq as a brother, not as a lover—just as he loved her as a sister. Plus, he had his mysterious dancer, she added wryly, as she poured herself another cup of tea in a clean cup, then reached for a slice of toast.

'You look pale. What's wrong?' Glancing up, she found Hassan's eyes were narrowed on her profile.

'She hates surprises.' Rafiq offered a reply.

'Ah. So I am out of favour,' Hassan drawled. 'Like the milk and the butter…' he added with the sharp eyes that should have been gold, like a falcon's, not a bottomless black that made her feel as if she could sink right into them and never have to come back out again.

'The milk was off, it turned my stomach, so I decided not to risk it or the butter,' she said, explaining the reason why she was sipping clear tea and nibbling on a piece of dry toast.

Keeping dairy produce fresh was an occupational hazard in hot climates, so Hassan didn't bother to question her answer—though Leona did a moment later when a pot of fresh coffee arrived for Hassan and the aroma sent her stomach dipping all over again.

Hassan saw the way she pushed her plate away and sat back in the chair with the paleness more pronounced, and had to ask himself if her pallor was more to do with anxiety than a problem with the milk. Maybe he should not be teasing her like this. Maybe no surprise, no matter how pleasant was going to merit putting her through yet more stress. He glanced at his watch. Ten more minutes. Was it worth him hanging on that long?

'You look stunning,' he murmured.

She turned her head, her wonderful hair floating out around her sun-kissed shoulders and the perfect heart-shape of her face. Her eyes were like emeralds, to match the one she wore on her finger, glowing with a passion she could never quite subdue no matter how low she was feeling. Kiss me, her small, soft, slightly sulky mouth seemed to say.

'I am *de trop*.' Rafiq broke through the moment and rose

to his feet. 'I will go and awaken Samir and drag him to the gym for an hour before I allow him breakfast.'

Neither bothered to answer even if they heard him, which Rafiq seriously doubted as he went to leave. Then a sound beyond the canvas awning caught his attention, diverting him towards the rail. A car was coming down the concrete quay towards them, its long black sleekly expensive lines giving him a good idea as to who was inside it.

This time he made sure he commanded attention by lightly touching Hassan's shoulder. 'Your surprise is arriving,' he told him, then left as Hassan stirred himself and Leona blinked herself back from wherever she had gone to.

Getting up, Hassan went to capture one of her hands and urged her out of her chair. 'Come,' he said, and keeping hold of her hand walked them down the stairs, across the foyer, out onto the shade deck and to the rail beside the gangway, just in time to watch a beautiful creature with pale blonde hair step out of the car and onto the quayside.

Beside him he felt Leona's breath catch on a gasp, felt the pulse in her wrist begin to race. 'Evie,' she whispered. 'And Raschid,' she added as Sheikh Raschid Al-Kadah uncoiled his long lean body out of the car.

'They're sailing with us?' Now her eyes were shining with true pleasure, Hassan noted with deep satisfaction. Now she was looking at him as if he was the most wonderful guy in the world, instead of the most painful to be around.

'Will their presence make your miserable lot easier to bear?'

Her reply was swift and uninhibited. She fell upon him with a kiss he would have given half of his wealth for. Though it did not need wealth, only the appearance of her closest friend and conspirator against these—arrogant Arabian men, as she and Evie liked to call Raschid and himself.

'After six years, I would have expected the unrestrained passion to have cooled a little,' a deep smooth, virtually accent-free voice mocked lazily.

'Says the man with his son clutched in one arm and his daughter cradled in the other,' mocked a lighter, drier voice.

Son and daughter. Hassan stiffened in shock, for he had not expected the Al-Kadahs to bring along their children on this cruise. Leona, on the other hand, was pulling away from him, turning away from him—hiding away from him? Had his pleasant surprise turned into yet another disaster? He turned to see what she was seeing and felt his chest tighten so fiercely it felt as if it was snapping in two. For there stood Raschid, as proud as any man could be, with his small son balanced on his arm while the beautiful Evie was in the process of gently relieving him of his small pink three-month-old daughter.

They began walking up the gangway towards them, and it was his worst nightmare unfolding before his very eyes, because there were tears in Leona's as she went to meet them. Real tears—bright tears when she looked down at the baby then up at Evangeline Al-Kadah before, with aching description, she simply took the other woman in her arms and held her.

Raschid was watching them, smiling, relaxed while he waited a few steps down the gangway for them to give him room to board the boat. He saw nothing painful in Leona's greeting, nor the way she broke away to gently touch a finger to the baby girl's petal soft cheek.

'I didn't know,' she was saying softly to Evie. 'Last time I saw you, you weren't even pregnant!'

'A lot can happen in a year,' Raschid put in dryly, bringing Leona's attention his way.

The tableau shifted. Evie moved to one side to allow her husband to step onto the deck so he could put his son to the ground, leaving his arms free to greet Leona properly. 'And aren't you just as proud as a peacock?' She laughed, defying the Arab male-female don't-touch convention by going straight into Raschid's arms.

What was wrong with Hassan? Leona wondered, realising that he hadn't moved a single muscle to come and greet their latest guests. She caught his eye over one of Raschid's broad shoulders, sent him a frowning look that told him to pull himself together. By the time he was greeting Evie Leona was squatting down to say hello to the little boy who now clutched his mother's skirt for safety. Dark like his father; golden-eyed like his father. The fates had been kind to these two people by allowing them to produce a son in Raschid's image and a daughter who already looked as if she was going to be a mirror of her mother.

'Hello, Hashim.' She smiled gently. They had met before but she was sure the small boy would not remember. 'Does that thumb taste very nice?'

He nodded gravely and stuck the thumb just that quarter inch further between sweetly pouting lips.

'My name is Leona,' she told him. 'Do you think we can be friends?'

'Red,' he said around the thumb, looking at her hair. 'Sunshine.'

'Thank you.' She laughed. 'I see you are going to be a dreadful flirt, like your papa.'

Mentioning his papa sent the toddler over to Raschid, where he begged to be picked up again. Raschid swung him up without pausing in his conversation with Hassan, as if it was the most natural thing in the world for him to have his son on his arm.

Tears hit again. Leona blinked them away. Hassan gave a tense shift of one shoulder and in the next moment his arm was resting across her shoulders. He was smiling at Evie, at her baby, at Raschid. But when Leona noticed that he was not allowing himself to so much as glance at Raschid's son it finally hit her what was the matter with him. Hassan could not bear to look at what Raschid had, that which he most coveted.

Her heart dropped to her stomach to make her feel sick again. The two men had been good friends since—for ever. Their countries lay side by side. And they shared so many similarities in their lives that Leona would have wagered everything that nothing could drive a wedge between their friendship.

But a desire for what one had that the other did not, in the shape of a boy-child, could do it, she realised, and had to move away from Hassan because she just couldn't bear to be near him and feel that need pulsing in him.

'May I?' she requested of Evie, holding out her arms for the baby.

Evie didn't hesitate in handing the baby over. Soft and light and so very fragile. It was like cradling an angel. 'How old is she?' she asked.

'Three months,' Evie supplied. 'As quiet as a mouse, as sweet as honey—and called Yamila Lucinda after her two grandmothers, but we call her Lucy because it's cute.'

At the sound of her mother's voice, Lucy opened her eyes to reveal two perfect amethysts the same as Evie's, and Leona found herself swallowing tears again.

You're so lucky, she wanted to say, but remarks like that were a potential minefield for someone in her situation. So she contented herself with lifting the baby up so she could feel her soft cheek against her own and hoped that no one noticed the small prick of tears she had to blink away.

A minute later and other guests began appearing on the shade deck to find out who else had joined them. Sheikh Raschid earned himself looks of wary surprise from some. From all he was awarded the respect accorded to a man who held absolute rule in his own Gulf state of Behran. His children brought down other barriers; the fact that Evie had achieved what Leona had not, in the shape of her small son, earned her warm smiles instead of stiffly polite ones that conveyed disapproval. Still, most of the tension from the evening before melted away in the face of the newcomers, and Leona was deeply grateful to them for succeeding in neutralising the situation.

When it was decided that they would move up to the sun deck, with its adjoining salon, to take refreshment and talk in comfort, Leona quickly shifted herself into hostess mode

and led the way upstairs with her small bundle in her arms
and her husband walking at her shoulder.

He didn't speak, and she could sense the same mood about
him he had donned when he'd come face to face with
Raschid and his son. It hurt. Though she strove not to show
it. But his manner made such a mockery out of everything
else he had said and done.

They arrived on the upper deck as the yacht slipped
smoothly from its moorings and began making its way towards the mouth of the Suez Canal. Medina Al-Mahmud
suddenly appeared in front of Leona and politely begged to
hold the baby. She was a small, slight woman with nervous
eyes and a defensive manner, but as Leona placed the little
girl in her arms Medina sent her a sympathetic look which
almost broke her composure in two.

She did not want people's pity. Oh, how she had come to
hate it during her last year in Rahman when the rumours
about her had begun flying. With a desperate need of something else to do other than stand here feeling utterly useless,
she walked into the salon to pick up the internal phone and
order refreshments.

It was really very bad timing for Hassan to follow her. 'I
must offer you my deepest apologies,' he announced so
stiffly it was almost an insult. 'When I arranged this surprise
for you I did not expect the Al-Kadahs to bring their children
with them.'

She was appalled to realise that even Hassan believed her
an object of such pity. 'Oh, stop being so ultra-sensitive,'
she snapped. 'Do you really believe that I could resent them
their beautiful children because I cannot have them for myself?'

'Don't say that!' he snapped back. 'It is not true, though
you drive me insane by insisting it is so!'

'And you stop burying your head in the sand, Hassan,' she
returned. 'Because we both know that you know it is you
who lies to yourself!'

With that she stalked off, leaving him to simmer in his

own frustration while she went to check that the accommo-
dation could stretch to two more guests than they had expected. Faysal already had the matter in hand, she discovered, finding several people hurriedly making ready a pair of
adjoining suites, while others unpacked enough equipment,
brought by the Al-Kadahs, to keep an army of young children content.

On her way back upstairs she met Rafiq and Samir. Rafiq
studied her narrowly, his shrewd gaze not missing the continuing paleness in her face. He was probably questioning
whether one sniff at suspect milk could upset her stomach
for so long when in actual fact it had never been the milk,
she had come to realise, but sheer anxiety and stress.

Samir, on the other hand, noticed nothing but a target for
his wit. By the time the three of them had joined the others,
Samir had her laughing over a heavily embroidered description of himself being put through the agonies of hell in the
gym by a man so fit it was a sin.

After that she played the circulating hostess to the hilt and
even endured a whole ten minutes sitting with Zafina listening to her extol the virtues of her daughter, Nadira. Then
Evie rescued her by quietly asking if she would show her to
their room, because the baby needed changing.

With Hashim deciding to come with them, they went down
to the now beautifully prepared twin cabins and a dark-eyed
little nurse Evie had brought with them appeared, to take the
children into the other room. The moment the two women
were alone Evie swung round on Leona and said, 'Right,
let's hear it. Why did Hassan virtually beg and bribe us to
come along on this trip?'

At which point, Leona simply broke down and wept out
the whole sorry story. By the time she had hiccuped to a
finish they were curled up on the bed and Evie was gently
stroking her hair.

'I think you are here to make me feel better.' She finally
answered Evie's original question. 'Because anyone with
eyes can see that the Al-Mahmuds and the Al-Yasins wish

me on another planet entirely. Hassan doesn't know that I've always known that Nadira Al-Yasin is the people's preferred wife for him.'

'I've been there. I know the feeling,' Evie murmured understandingly. 'I suppose she's beautiful, biddable and loves children.'

Leona nodded on a muffled sob. 'I've met her once or twice. She's quite sweet,' she reluctantly confessed.

'Just right for Hassan, I suppose.'

'Yes,'

'And, of course, you are not.'

Leona shook her head.

'So why are you here, then?' Evie challenged.

'You tell me,' she suggested, finding strength in anger and pulling herself into a sitting position on the bed. 'Because I don't know! Hassan says I am here for this reason, then he changes it to another. He is stubborn and devious and an absolute expert at plucking at my heart strings! His father is ill and I adore that old man so he uses him to keep me dancing to his secret tune!'

'Raschid's father died in his arms while I held Raschid in my arms,' Evie told her sadly. 'Wretched though it was, I would not have been anywhere else. He needed me. Hassan needs you too.'

'Oh, don't defend him,' Leona protested, 'It makes me feel mean, yet I know I would have gone to his father like a shot with just that request. I didn't need all of this other stuff to make me do it.'

'But maybe Hassan needed this other stuff to let him make you do it.'

'I'm going to sit you at the dinner table between Mrs Yasin and Mrs Mahmud tonight if you don't stop trying to be reasonable,' Leona said warningly.

'Okay, you've made your point,' Evie conceded. 'You need a loyal champion, not a wise one.' Then, with a complete change of manner, 'So get yourself into the bathroom and tidy yourself up before we go and fight the old dragons together.'

Leona began to smile. 'Now you're talking,' she enthused, and, stretching out a long leg, she rose from the bed a different person than the one who'd slumped down on it minutes ago. 'I'm glad you're here, Evie,' she murmured huskily.

It was a remark she could have repeated a hundred times over during the following days when everyone did try to appear content to simply enjoy the cruise with no underlying disputes to spoil it.

But in truth many undercurrents were at work. In the complicated way of Arab politics, there was no natural right to succession in Rahman. First among equals was the Arab way of describing a collective of tribe leaders amongst which one is considered the most authoritative. The next leader did not necessarily have to be the son of the one preceding him, but choice became an open issue on which all heads of the family must agree.

In truth everyone knew that Hassan was the only sensible man for the job simply because he had been handling the modern thrusts of power so successfully for the last five years as his father's health had begun to fail. No one wanted to tip the balance. As it stood, the other families had lived well and prospered under Al-Qadim rule. Rahman was a respected country in Arabia. Landlocked though it was, the oil beneath its desert was rich and in plenty, and within its borders were some of the most important oases that other, more favourably placed countries, did not enjoy.

But just as the sands shifted, so did opinions. Al-Mahmud and Al-Yasin might have lived well and prospered under thirty years of Al-Qadim rule, but they had disapproved of Hassan's choice of wife from the beginning. Though they could not fault the dedication Hassan's wife had applied to her role, nor ignore the respect she had earned from the Rahman people, she was frail of body. She had produced no sons in five years of marriage, and then had made Hassan appear weak to his peers when she'd walked away from him of her own volition. Divorce should have followed swiftly. Hassan had refused to discuss it as an option. Therefore, a second wife should have been chosen. Hassan's refusal to pander to what he called the ways of the old guard had incensed many. Not least Sheikh Abdul Al-Yasin who had not stopped smarting from the insult he'd received when Hassan had not chosen his daughter, Nadira, who had been primed from birth to take the role.

With Hassan's father's health failing fast, Sheikh Abdul had seen an opportunity to redress this insult. All it required was for Hassan to agree to take on a second wife in order to maintain the delicate balance between families. It was that simple. Everyone except Hassan agreed that his marriage to Nadira Al-Yasin would form an alliance that would solve everyone's problems. Hassan could keep his first wife. No one was asking him to discard this beautiful but barren woman. But his first son would come from the womb of Nadira Al-Yasin, which was all that really mattered.

The alternatives? Sheikh Jibril Al-Mahmud had a son who could be considered worthy of taking up the mantle Hassan's father would leave vacant. And no one could afford to ignore Sheikh Imran Al-Mukhtar and his son, Samir. Samir might be too young to take on the mantle of power but his father was not.

This, however only dealt with the male perspective. As the sheikhs fought their war with words on each other during long discussions, ensconced in one of the staterooms, the women were waging a similar war for their own reasons. Zafina Al-Yasin wanted Leona out and her daughter, Nadira, in. Since Hassan was not allowing this, then she would settle for her daughter taking second place. For the power lay in the sons born in a marriage, not the wives. So critical remarks were dropped at every opportunity to whittle away at Leona's composure and a self-esteem that was already fragile due to her inability to give Hassan what he needed most in this world.

In the middle of it all stood Sheikh Raschid and his wife, Evie offering positive proof that west could successfully join with east. For Behran had gone from strength to strength since their marriage and was fast becoming one of the most influential States in Arabia. But they had a son. It was the cog on which everything else rotated.

It took two days to navigate the Suez Canal, and would take another five to cross the Red Sea to the city of Jeddah on the coast of Saudi Arabia. By the time they had reached the end of the Canal, battle lines had been clearly marked for those times when the war of words would rage or a truce would be called. Mornings were truce times, when everyone more or less did their own thing and the company could even be called pleasant.

In the afternoons most people took a siesta, unless Samir grew restless and chivvied the others towards more enjoyable pursuits.

'Just look at them,' Evie murmured indulgently one afternoon as they stood watching Samir, Rafiq, Raschid and Hassan jet-skiing the ocean like reckless idiots, criss-crossing each other's wash with a daring that sometimes caught the breath. 'They're like little boys with exciting new toys.'

They came back to the boat, refreshed, relaxed—and ready to begin the first wave of strikes when the men gathered to drink coffee in one of the staterooms while the women occupied another.

Dinner called a second truce. After dinner, when another split of the sexes occurred, hostilities would resume until someone decided to call it a day and went to bed.

Bed was a place you could neither describe as a place of war nor truce. It gave you a sanctuary in which you had the chance to vent all of the things you had spent the day suppressing. But when the person in the bed with you saw you as much the enemy as every one else did, then you were in deep trouble. As Hassan acknowledged every time he slid into bed beside Leona and received the cold shoulder if he so much as attempted to touch her or speak.

She was angry with him for many reasons, but angriest most for some obscure point he had not managed to expose. He was aware that this situation was difficult, that she would rather be anywhere else other than trapped on this yacht right now. He knew she was unhappy, that she was only just managing to hide that from everyone else. That she was eating little and looking contradictorily pale when in truth her skin was taking on a deeper golden hue with every passing day. He knew that Zafina and Medina used any opportunity presented to them to compare her situation unfavourably with Evie's. And he wished Raschid had shown some sensitivity to that prospect when he'd made the decision to bring his children along!

The children were a point of conflict he could not seem to deal with. This evening, for instance, when Raschid had brought his son into the salon to say goodnight to everyone, Hashim had run the length of the room with his arms open wide in demand for a hug from Leona. She had lifted him up in her arms and received all of his warm kisses to her face with smiles of pleasure while inside, Hassan knew, the ache of empty wishes must be torture for her.

When she hurt, he hurt. When he had no remedy to ease that pain, he had to turn away from its source or risk revealing to her the emptiness of helplessness he suffered whenever he saw her hugging a son that was not their own.

But in trying to protect Leona from himself he had forgotten the other pairs of eyes watching him. The Al-Mahmuds and the Al-Yasins had seen, read and drawn their own conclusions.

'A sad sight, is it not?' Abdul had dared to say.

Leona had heard him, had known what he'd been referring to, and had been shunning Hassan ever since.

'Talk to me, for Allah's sake.' He sighed into the darkness.

'Find another bed to sleep in.'

Well, they were words, he supposed, then sighed again, took the bull by the horns and pushed himself up to lean over her, then tugged her round to face him. 'What is it that you want from me?' he demanded. 'I am trying my best to make this work for us!'

Her eyes flicked open; it was like gazing into pools of broken ice. 'Why go to all this trouble when I am still going to leave you flat the first moment I know I can do it without hurting your father?'

'Why?' he challenged.

'We've already been through the *whys* a hundred times! They haven't changed just because you have decided to play the warlord and win the battle against your rotten underlings without giving an inch to anyone!'

'Warlord?' His brow arched. 'How very pagan.' He made sure she knew he liked the sound of that title in a very physical way.

'Oh, get off me,' she snapped, gave a push and rolled free of him, coming to her feet by the bed. Her hair floated everywhere, and the cream silk pyjamas shimmied over her slender figure as she walked down the room and dumped herself into one of the chairs, then dared to curl up in it as if he would allow her to sleep there!

'Come back here, Leona,' he commanded wearily.

'I regret ever agreeing to be here,' she answered huskily.

Husky meant tears. Tears made him want to curse for making a joke of what they had been talking about when any fool would have known it was no time for jokes! On yet another sigh he got out of the bed, then trod in her footsteps and went to squat down in front of her.

'I'm sorry,' he said, 'that this situation is so difficult for you. But my father insisted that the family heads must talk to each other. I have no will to refuse him because in truth his reasons are wise. You know I have no automatic right to succession. I must win the support of the other family leaders.'

'Stop being so stubborn and just let me go and you would not have to win over anyone,' she pointed out.

'You know...' he grimaced '...I think you are wrong

there. I think that underneath all the posturing they want me to fight this battle and win, to prove the strength of my resolve.'

She brushed a tear off her cheek. Hassan had wanted to do it for her, but instinct was warning him not to. 'Tonight Zafina asked me outright if I had any idea of the life I was condemning you to if I held onto a marriage destined to have no children.'

His eyes flashed with raw anger, his lips pressing together on an urge to spit out words that would make neither of them feel any better. But he made a mental note that from tomorrow Leona went nowhere without himself or Rafiq within hearing.

'And I saw your face, Hassan,' she went on unsteadily. 'I heard what Abdul said to you and I know why he said it. So why are you being so stubborn about something we both know is—'

He shut her up in the most effective way he knew. Mouth to mouth, tongue to tongue, words lost in the heat of a much more productive form of communication. She fought him for a few brief seconds, then lost the battle when her flailing fingers made contact with his naked flesh.

He had no clothes on, she had too many, but flesh-warmed silk against naked skin achieved a sensual quality he found very pleasurable as he lifted her up and settled her legs around his hips.

'You are such an ostrich,' she threw into his face as he carried her back to bed. 'How long do you think you can go on ignoring what—!'

He used the same method to shut her up again. By then he was standing by the bed with her fingernails digging into his shoulders, her hair surrounding him and her long legs clinging to his waist with no indication that they were going to let go. If he tried for a horizontal position he would risk hurting her while she held him like this.

So—who needed a bed? he thought with a shrug as his fingers found the elastic waistband to her pyjama bottoms and pushed the silk far enough down her thighs to gain him access to what he wanted the most. She groaned as he eased himself into her, and the kiss deepened into something else.

Fevered was what it was. Fevered and hot and a challenge to how long he could maintain his balance as he stood there with his hands spanning her slender buttocks, squeezing to increase the frictional pleasure, and no way—no way— would he have believed three nights without doing this could leave him so hungry. Twelve months without doing this had not affected him as badly.

'You're shaking.'

She'd noticed. He wasn't surprised. He wasn't just shaking, he was out of control, and he could no longer maintain this position without losing his dignity as well as his mind. So he lowered her to the bed with as much care as he could muster, pushed her hair from her face and stared blackly into her eyes.

'You tell me how I deny myself this above all things?' he demanded. 'You, only you, can do this to me. It is only you I want to do it with.'

The words were spoken between fierce kisses, between possessive thrusts from his hips. Leona touched his face, touched his mouth, touched his eyes with her eyes. 'I'm so very sorry,' she whispered tragically.

It was enough to drive an already driven man insane. He withdrew, got up, swung away and strode into the bathroom, slammed shut the door then turned to slam the flat of his palm against the nearest wall. Empty silences after the loving he had learned to deal with, but tragic apologies in the middle were one large step too far!

Why had she said it? She hadn't meant to say it! It was just one of those painful little things that had slipped out because she had seen he was hurting, and the look had reminded her of the look he had tried to hide from her when she had been cuddling Hashim.

Oh, what were they doing to each other? Leona asked

herself wretchedly. And scrambled to her feet as the sickness she had been struggling with for days now came back with a vengeance, leaving her with no choice but to make a run for the bathroom with the hope that he hadn't locked the door.

With one hand over her mouth and the other trying to recover her slipping pyjama bottoms, she reached the door just as it flew open to reveal a completely different Hassan than the one who had stormed in there only seconds ago.

'You may have your wish,' he informed her coldly. 'As soon as it is safe for me to do so, I will arrange a divorce. Now I want nothing more to do with you.'

With that he walked away, having no idea that her only response was to finish what she had been intending to do and make it to the toilet bowl before she was sick.

CHAPTER EIGHT

LEONA was asleep when Hassan let himself back into the room the next morning. She was still asleep when, showered and dressed, he left the room again half an hour later, and in a way he was glad.

He had spent the night stretched out on a lounger on the shade deck, alternating between feeling angry enough to stand by every word he had spoken and wanting to go back and retract what he had left hanging in the air.

And even now, hours later, he was not ready to choose which way he was going to go. He'd had enough of people tugging on his heartstrings; he'd had enough of playing these stupid power games.

He met Rafiq on his way up to the sun deck. 'Set up a meeting,' he said. 'Ten o'clock in my private office. We are going for broke.'

Rafiq sent him one of his steady looks, went to say something, changed his mind, and merely nodded his head.

Samir was already at the breakfast table, packing food away at a pace that made Hassan feel slightly sick—a combination of no sleep and one too many arguments, he told himself grimly.

Leona still hadn't put in an appearance by the time everyone else had joined them and finished their breakfast. Motioning the steward over, he instructed him to ring the suite.

'I'll go,' Evie offered, and got up, leaving her children to Raschid's capable care.

And he was capable. In fact it irritated Hassan how capable his friend was at taking care of his two children. How

120

did he run a Gulf state the size of Behran and find time to learn how to deal with babies?

The sun was hot, the sky was blue and here he was, he acknowledged, sitting here feeling like a grey day in London.

'Hassan…'

'Hmm?' Glancing up, he realised that Sheikh Imran had been talking to him and he hadn't heard a single word that he had said.

'Rafiq tells us you have called a meeting for ten o'clock'

'Yes.' He glanced at his watch, frowned and stood up. 'If you will excuse me, this is the time I call my father.'

To reach his office required him to pass by his suite door. It was closed. He hesitated, wondering whether or not to go in and at least try to make his peace. But Evie was in there, he remembered, and walked on, grimly glad of the excuse not to have to face that particular problem just now. For he had bigger fish to fry this morning.

Faysal was already in the office. 'Get my father on the phone for me, Faysal,' he instructed. 'Then set the other room up ready for a meeting.'

'It is to be today, sir?' Faysal questioned in surprise.

'Yes, today. In half an hour. My father, Faysal,' he prompted before the other man could say any more. He glanced at his watch again as Faysal picked up the telephone. Had Leona stayed in their suite because she didn't want to come face to face with him?

But Leona had not stayed in their suite because she was sulking, as Hassan so liked to call it. She was ill, and didn't want anyone to know.

'Don't you dare tell anyone,' she warned Evie. 'I'll be all right in a bit. It just keeps happening, and then it goes away again.'

'How long?' Evie looked worried.

'A few days.' Leona shrugged. 'I don't think I've got anything your children might catch, Evie,' she then anxiously assured her. 'I'm just—stressed out, that's all.'

'Stressed out.' Evie was looking at her oddly.

'It's playing havoc with my stomach.' Leona nodded and took another sip of the bottled water Evie had opened for her. 'Who would not be feeling sick if they were stuck on this boat with a load of people they liked as little as those people liked them? You and your family excluded, of course,' she then added belatedly.

'Oh, of course.' Evie nodded and sat down on the edge of the bed, a bed with one half that had not been slept in. Hassan had not come back last night, and Leona was glad that he hadn't.

'I hate men,' she announced huskily.

'You mean you hate one man in particular.'

'I'll be glad when this is over and he just lets me go.'

'Do you really think that is likely?' Evie mocked. 'Hassan is an Arab and they give up on nothing. Arrogant, possessive, stubborn, selfish and sweet,' she listed ruefully. 'It is the moments of sweetness that are their saving grace, I find.'

'You're lucky, you've got a nice one.'

'He wasn't nice at all on the day I sent him packing,' Evie recalled. 'In fact it was the worst moment of my life when he turned to leave with absolutely no protest. I knew it was the end. I'd seen it carved into his face like words set in stone…'

'I know,' Leona whispered miserably. 'I've seen the look myself…'

Evie had seen the same look on Hassan's face at the breakfast table. 'Oh, Leona.' She sighed. 'The two of you have got to stop beating each other up like this. You love each other. Can't that be enough?'

Raschid was not in agreement with Hassan's timing. 'Think about this,' he urged. 'We have too much time before we reach dry land. Time for them to fester on their disappointment.'

'I need this settled,' Hassan grimly insisted. 'Leona is a mess. The longer I let the situation ride the more hesitant I appear. Both Abdul and Zafina Al-Yasin are becoming so over-confident that they think they may say what they please. My father agrees. It shall be done with today. *Inshallah*,' he concluded.

'*Inshallah*, indeed,' Raschid murmured ruefully, and went away to prepare what he had been brought here specifically to say.

An hour later Evie was with her children, Medina and Zafina were seated quietly in one of the salons sipping coffee while they awaited the outcome of the meeting taking place on the deck below, and Leona and Samir were kitting up to go jet-skiing when Sheikh Raschid Al-Kadah decided it was time for him to speak.

'I have listened to your arguments with great interest and some growing concern,' he smoothly began. 'Some of you seem to be suggesting that Hassan should make a choice between his country and his western wife. I find this a most disturbing concept—not only because I have a western wife myself, but because forward-thinking Arabs might be setting such outmoded boundaries upon their leaders for the sake of what?'

'The blood line,' Abdul said instantly.

Some of the others shifted uncomfortably. Raschid looked into the face of each and every one of them and challenged them to agree with Sheikh Abdul. It would be an insult to himself, his wife and children if they did so. None did.

'The blood line was at risk six years ago, Abdul.' He smoothly directed his answer at the man who had dared to offer such a dangerous reason. 'When Hassan married, his wife was accepted by you all. What has changed?'

'You misunderstand, Raschid,' Jibril Al-Mahmud quickly inserted, eager to soothe the ruffled feathers of the other man. 'My apologies, Hassan, for feeling pressed to say this.' He bowed. 'But it is well known throughout Rahman that your most respected wife cannot bear a child.'

'This is untrue, but please continue with your hypothesis,' Hassan invited calmly.

Flustered, Jibril looked back at Raschid. 'Even in your

country a man is allowed, if not expected, to take a second wife if the first is—struggling to give him sons,' he pointed out. 'We beg Hassan only take a second wife to secure the *family* line.' Wisely, he omitted the word 'blood'.

'Hassan?' Raschid looked to him for an answer.

Hassan shook his head. 'I have the only wife I need,' he declared.

'And if Allah decides to deny you sons, what then?'

'Then control passes on to my successor. I do not see the problem.'

'The problem is that your stance makes a mockery of everything we stand for as Arabs,' Abdul said impatiently. 'You have a duty to secure the continuance of the Al-Qadim name. Your father agrees. The old ones agree. I find it insupportable that you continue to insist on giving back nothing for the honour of being your father's son!'

'I give back my right to succession,' Hassan countered. 'I am prepared to step down and let one or other of you here take my place. There,' he concluded with a flick of the hand, 'it is done. You may now move on to discuss my father's successor without me...'

'One moment, Hassan...' It was Raschid who stopped him from rising. Worked in and timed to reach this point in proceedings, he said, 'I have some objections to put forward against your decision.'

Hassan returned to his seat. Raschid nodded his gratitude for this, then addressed the table as a whole. 'Rahman's land borders my land. Your oil pipeline runs beneath Behran soil and mixes with my oil in our co-owned holding tanks when it reaches the Gulf. And the old ones criss-cross our borders from oasis to oasis with a freedom laid down in a treaty drawn up and signed by Al-Kadah and Al-Qadim thirty years ago. So tell me,' he begged, 'with whom am I expected to renegotiate this treaty when an Al-Qadim is no longer in a position to honour his side of our bargain?'

It was an attack on all fronts. For Rahman was landlocked. It needed Behran to get its oil to the tankers that moored up at its vast terminals. The treaty was old and the tariffs laid down in it had not been changed in those thirty years Raschid had mentioned. Borders were mere lines on maps the old ones were free to ignore as they roamed the desert with their camel trains.

'There is no question of altering the balance of power here in Rahman,' It was Sheikh Jibril Al-Mahmud who declaimed the suggestion. He looked worried. Crown Prince Raschid Al-Kadah was not known as a bluffing man. 'Hassan has our complete loyalty, respect and support.'

'Ah,' Raschid said. 'Then I am mistaken in what I have been hearing here. My apologies.' He bowed. 'I believed I was hearing Hassan about to step down as his father's natural successor.'

'Indeed no such thing ever crossed our minds.' You could almost see Sheikh Jibril shifting his position into the other camp as he spoke. 'We are merely concerned about future successors and question whether it is not time for Hassan to consider taking steps to—'

'As the old ones would say,' Raschid smoothly cut in, 'time is but a grain of sand that shifts in accordance with the wind and the will of Allah.'

'*Inshallah*,' Sheikh Jibril agreed, bringing Sheikh Abdul's house of cards tumbling down.

'Thank you,' Hassan murmured to Raschid a few minutes later, when the others had left them. 'I am in your debt.'

'There is no debt,' Raschid denied. 'I have no wish to see the spawn of Sheikh Abdul Al-Yasin develop in to the man who will then deal with my son. But, as a matter of interest only, who is your successor?'

'Rafiq,' Hassan replied.

'But he does not want the job.'

'He will nonetheless acquire it,' Hassan said grimly.

'Does he know?'

'Yes. We have already discussed it.'

Raschid nodded thoughtfully, then offered a grim smile.

'Now all you have to do, my friend, is try to appear happy that you have achieved your goal.'

It was Hassan's cue to begin smiling, but instead he released a heavy sigh and went to stand by the window. Outside, skimming across the glass-smooth water, he could see two jet-skis teasing each other. Leona's hair streamed out behind her like a glorious banner as she stood, half bent at the knees, turning the machine into a neat one-hundred-and-eighty-degree-spin in an effort to chase after the reckless Samir.

'The victory could be an empty one in the end,' he murmured eventually. 'For I do not think she will stay.'

Raschid's silence brought Hassan's head round. What he saw etched into the other man's face said it all for him. 'You don't think she will, either, do you?' he stated huskily.

'Evie and I discussed this,' Raschid confessed. 'We swapped places with you and Leona, if you like. And quite honestly, Hassan, her answer made my blood run cold.'

Hassan was not surprised by that. East meets west, he mused as he turned back to the window. Pride against pride. The love of a good, courageous woman against the—

'In the name of Allah,' he suddenly rasped out as he watched Leona's jet-ski stop so suddenly that she was thrown right over the front of it.

'What?' Raschid got to his feet.

'She hit something,' he bit out, remaining still for a moment, waiting for her to come up. It didn't happen. His heart began to pound, ringing loudly in his ears as he turned and began to run. With Raschid close on his heels he took the stairs two at a time, then flung himself down the next set heading for the rear of the boat where the back let down to form a platform into the water. Rafiq was already there, urgently lowering another jet ski into the water. His taut face said it all; Leona still had not reappeared. Samir had not even noticed; he was too busy making a wide, arching turn way out.

Without hesitation he wrenched the jet-ski from Rafiq and

was speeding off towards his wife before his brother had realised what he had done. Teeth set, eyes sharp, he made an arrow-straight track towards her deadly still jet-ski as behind him the yacht began sounding its horn in a warning call to Samir. The sound brought everyone to the boatside, to see what was going on.

By the time Hassan came up on Leona's jet-ski, Rafiq was racing after him on another one and Samir was heading towards them at speed. No one else moved or spoke or even breathed as they watched Hassan take a leaping dive off his moving machine and disappear into the deep blue water. Three minutes had past, maybe four, and Hassan could not understand why her buoyancy aid had not brought her to the surface.

He found out why the moment he broke his dive down and twisted full circle in the water. A huge piece of wood, like the beam from an old fishing boat, floated just below the surface—tangled with fishing net. It was the net she was caught in, a slender ankle, a slender wrist, and she was frantically trying to free herself.

As he swam towards her, he saw the panic in her eyes, the belief that she was going to die. With his own lungs already wanting to burst, he reached down to free her foot first, then began hauling her towards the surface even as he wrenched free her wrist.

White, he was white with panic, overwhelmed by shock and gasping greedily for breath. She burst out crying, coughing, spluttering, trying desperately to fill her lungs through racking sobs that tore him to bits. Neither had even noticed the two other jet-skis warily circling them or that Raschid and a crewman were heading towards them in the yacht's emergency inflatable.

'Why is it you have to *do* this to me?' he shouted at her furiously.

'Hassan,' someone said gruffly. He looked up, saw his brother's face, saw Samir looking like a ghost, saw the inflatable almost upon them, then saw—really saw—the woman he held crushed in his arms. After that the world took on a blur as Rafiq and Samir joined them in the water and helped to lift Leona into the boat. Hassan followed, then asked Raschid and the crewman to bring in the other two men on the jet-skis. As soon as the jet-skis left the inflatable, he turned it round and, instead of making for the yacht, he headed out in the Red Sea.

Leona didn't notice, she was lying in a huddle still sobbing her heart out on top of a mound of towels someone had had the foresight to toss into the boat, and he was shaking from teeth to fingertips. His mind was shot, his eyes blinded by an emotion he had never experienced before in his life.

When he eventually stopped the boat in the middle of nowhere, he just sat there and tried hard to calm whatever it was that was raging inside of him while Leona tried to calm her frightened tears.

'You know,' he muttered after a while, 'for the first time since I was a boy, I think I am going to weep. You have no idea what you do to me, no idea at all. Sometimes I wonder if you even care.'

'It was an accident,' she whispered hoarsely

'So was the trip on the gangway! So was the headlong fall down the stairs! What difference does it make if it was an accident? You still have no idea what you do to me!'

Sitting up, she plucked up one the towels and wrapped it around her shivering frame.

'Are you listening to me?' he grated.

'No,' she replied. 'Where are we?'

'In the middle of nowhere where I can shout if I want to, cry if I want to, and tell the rest of the world to get out of my life!' he raged. 'I am sick of other people meddling in it. I am sick of playing stupid, political games. And I am sick and tired of watching you do stupid madcap things just because you are angry with me!'

'Hassan—'

'What?' he lashed back furiously, black eyes burning,

body so taut it looked ready to snap in two. He was soaking
wet and he was trembling—not shivering like herself.

'I'm all right,' she told him gently.

He fell on her like a ravaging wolf, setting the tiny boat
rocking and not seeming to care if they both ended up in the
water again. 'Four minutes you were under the water—I
timed it!' he bit out between tense kisses.

'I'm accident prone; you know I am,' she reminded him.
'The first time we met I tripped over someone's foot and
landed on your lap.'

'No.' He denied it. 'I helped you there with a guiding
hand.'

She frowned. He grimaced. He had never admitted that
before. 'I had been watching you all evening, wondering how
I could get to meet you without making myself appear over-
eager. So it was an opportunity sent from Allah when you
tripped just in front of me.'

Leona let loose a small, tear-choked chuckle. 'I tripped in
front of you on purpose,' she confessed. 'Someone said you
were an Arabian sheikh, rich as sin, so I thought to myself.
That will do for me!'

'Liar,' he murmured.

'Maybe.' She smiled.

Then the teasing vanished from both of them. Eyes darkened, drew closer, then dived into each other's to dip into a
place so very special it actually hurt to make contact with so
much feeling at once.

'Don't leave me—ever.' He begged her promise.

Leona sighed as she ran her fingers through his wet hair.
Her throat felt tight and her heart felt heavy. 'I'm frightened
that one day you will change your mind about me and want
more from your life. Then what will I be left with?'

'Ethan Hayes is in love with you,' he said.

'What has that got to do with this?' She frowned. 'And,
no, he is not.'

'You are frightened I will leave you. Well, I am frightened

that you will one day see a normal man like Ethan and decide he has more to offer you than I ever can.'

'You are joking,' she drawled.

'No, I am not.' He sat up, long fingers reaching out to pluck absently at the ropework around the sides of the boat. 'What do I offer you beside a lot of personal restrictions, political games that can get nasty enough to put your well-being at risk, and a social circle of friends you would not pass the day with if you did not feel obliged to do so for my sake.'

'I liked most of our friends in Rahman,' she protested, sitting up to drape one of the towels around her head because the sun was too hot. 'Those I didn't like, you don't particularly like, and we only used to see them at formal functions.'

'Or when we became stuck on a boat with them with no means of escape.'

'Why are we having this conversation in this small boat in the middle of the Red Sea?' she questioned wearily.

'Where else?' He shrugged. 'In our stateroom where there is a convenient bed to divert us away from what needs to be said?'

'It's another abduction,' she murmured ruefully.

'You belong to me. A man cannot abduct what is already his.'

'And you're arrogant.' She sighed.

'Loving you is arrogant of me?' he challenged.

Leona just shook her head and used the corner of the towel to dry her wet face. Her fingers were trembling, and she was still having a struggle to calm her breathing. 'Last night you promised me a divorce.'

'Today I am taking that promise back.'

'Here…' she held her arm out towards him. '…can you do something about this?'

Part of the netting she had been tangled in was still clinging to her wrist. The delicate skin beneath it was red and chafed. 'I'm sorry I said what I did last night,' he murmured.

'I'm sorry I said what I did,' Leona returned. 'I didn't even mean it the way it came out. It's just that sometimes you look so very…'

'Children are a precious gift from Allah,' Hassan interrupted, dark head sombrely bent over his task. 'But so is love. Very few people are fortunate enough to have both, and most only get the children. If I had to choose then I would choose, to have love.'

'But you are an Arabian sheikh with a duty to produce the next successor to follow on from you, and the choice no longer belongs to you.'

'If we find we want children then we will get some,' he said complacently, lifting up her wrist to break the stubborn cord with the sharp snap of his teeth. 'IVF, adoption… But only if *we* want them.' He made that fine but important point. 'Otherwise let Rafiq do his bit for his country,' he concluded with an indifferent shrug.

'He would give you one of his stares if he heard you saying that.' Leona smiled.

'He is an Al-Qadim, though he chooses to believe he is not.'

'He's half-French.'

'I am one quarter Spanish, and one quarter Al-Kadah,' he informed her. 'You, I believe, are one half rampaging Celt. I do not see us ringing bells about it.'

'All right, I will stay,' she murmured.

Dark eyes shrouded by a troubled frown lifted to look at her. 'You mean stay as in for ever, no more argument?' He demanded clarification.

Reaching up, she stroked her fingers through his hair again. 'As in you've got me for good, my lord Sheikh,' she said soberly. 'Just make sure you don't make me regret it.'

'Huh.' The short laugh was full of bewildered incredulity. 'What suddenly brought on this change of heart?'

'The heart has always wanted to stay, it was the mind that was causing me problems. But…look at us, Hassan.' She sighed 'sitting out in the middle of the sea in a stupid little boat beneath the heat of a noon-day sun because we would rather be here, together like this, than anywhere else.' She gave him her eyes again, and what always happened to them happened when he looked deep inside. 'If you believe love can sustain us through whatever is waiting for us back there, then I am going to let myself believe it too.'

'Courage,' he murmured, reaching out to gently cup her cheek. 'I never doubted your courage.'

'No,' she protested when he went to kiss her. 'Not here, when I can feel about twenty pairs of eyes trained on us from the yacht.'

'Let them watch,' he decreed, and kissed her anyway. 'Now I want the privacy of our stateroom, with its very large bed,' he said as he drew away again.

'Then, let's go and find it.'

They were halfway back to the yacht before she remembered Samir telling her about the planned meeting. 'What happened?' she asked anxiously.

Hassan smiled a brief, not particularly pleased smile. 'I won the support I was looking for. The fight is over. Now we can begin to relax a little.'

As a statement of triumph, it didn't have much satisfaction running through it. Leona wanted to question him about it, but they were nearing the yacht, so she decided to wait until later because she could now clearly see the sea of faces watching their approach—some anxious, some curious, some wearing expressions that set her shivering all over again. Not everyone was relieved that Hassan had plucked her out of the ocean, she realised ruefully.

Rafiq and a crewman were waiting on the platform to help them back on board the yacht. 'I'll walk,' she insisted when Hassan went to lift her into his arms. 'I think I have looked foolish enough for one day.'

So they walked side by side through the boat, wrapped in towels over their wet clothing. Neither spoke, neither touched, and no one accosted them on their journey to their stateroom. The door shut them in. Hassan broke away from her side and strode into the bathroom. Leona followed, found the jets in the shower already running. She dropped the towels, Hassan silently helped her out of the buoyancy aid that had not been buoyant enough and tossed it in disgust to the tiled floor. Next came her tee shirt, her shorts, the blue one-piece swimsuit she was wearing beneath.

It was another of those calms before the storm, Leona recognised as she watched him drag his shirt off over his head and step out of the rest of his clothes. His face was composed, his manner almost aloof, and there wasn't a single cell in her body that wasn't charged, ready to accept what had to come.

Tall and dark, lean and sleek. 'In,' he commanded, holding open the shower-cubicle door so that she could step inside. He followed, closed the door. And as the white-tiled space engulfed them in steam he was reaching for her and engulfing her in another way.

Think of asking questions about how much he had conceded to win his support from the other sheikhs? Why think about anything when this was warm and soft and slow and so intense that the yacht could sink and they would not have noticed. This was love, a renewal of love; touching, tasting, living, breathing, feeling love. From the shower they took it with them to the bed, from there they took it with them into a slumber which filtered the rest of the day away.

Questions? Who needed questions when they had this depth of communication? No more empty silences between the loving. No more fights with each other or with themselves about the wiseness of being together like this. When she received him inside her she did so with her eyes wide open and brimming with love and his name sounding softly on her lips.

Beyond the room, in another part of the yacht, Raschid looked at Rafiq. 'Do you think he has realised yet that today's victory has only put Leona at greater risk from her enemies?' he questioned.

'Sheikh Abdul would be a fool to show his hand now, when he must know that Hassan has chosen to pretend he had no concept of his plot to take her.'

'I was not thinking of Abdul, but his ambitious wife,' Raschid murmured grimly. 'The woman wants to see her daughter in Leona's place. One only had to glimpse her expression when Hassan brought them back to the yacht to know that she has not yet had the sense to give up the fight...'

CHAPTER NINE

LEONA was thinking much the same thing when she found herself faced by Zafina later that evening.

Before the confrontation the evening had been surprisingly pleasant. Leona made light of her spill into the sea, and the others made light of the meeting that had taken place as if the battle, now decided, had given everyone the excuse to relax their guard.

It was only when the women left the men at the table after dinner that things took a nasty turn for the worse. Evie had gone to check on her children and Leona used the moment to pop back to the stateroom to freshen up. The last person she expected to see as she stepped out of the bathroom was Zafina Al-Yasin, standing there waiting for her.

Dressed in a traditional jewel-blue *dara'a* and matching *thobe* heavily embroidered with silver studs, Zafina was here to cause trouble. It did not take more than a glance into her black opal eyes to see that.

'You surprise me with your jollity this evening.' The older woman began her attack. 'On a day when your husband won all and you lost everything I believed you stood so proudly for, I would have expected to find you more subdued. It was only as I watched you laugh with our men that it occurred to me that maybe, with your unfortunate accident and Sheikh Hassan's natural concern for you, he has not made you fully aware of what it was he has agreed to today?'

Not at all sure where she was going to be led with this, Leona demanded cautiously, 'Are you implying that my husband has lied to me?'

'I would not presume to suggest such a thing,' Zafina denied with a slight bow of respect meant in honour of Hassan, not Leona herself. 'But he may have been a little...economical with some of the details in an effort to save you from further distress.'

'Something you are not prepared to be,' Leona assumed.

'I believe in telling the truth, no matter the pain it may course.'

Ah, Leona thought, the truth. Now there was an interesting concept.

'In the interest of fair play, I do feel that you should be fully informed so that you may make your judgements on your future with the full facts at hand.'

'Why don't you just get to the point of this conversation, Zafina?' Leona said impatiently.

'The point is…this…' Zafina replied, producing from inside the sleeve of her *dara'a* a piece of paper, which she then spread out on the bed.

Leona did not want to, but she made herself walk towards it, made herself look down. The paper bore the Al-Qadim seal of office. It bore the name of Sheikh Khalifa.

'What is it?' she asked, oddly unwilling to read the closely lined and detailed Arabian script that came beneath.

'A contract drawn up by Sheikh Khalifa himself, giving his blessing to the marriage between his son Sheikh Hassan and my daughter Nadira. This is my husband's copy. Sheikh Khalifa and Sheikh Hassan have copies of their own.'

'It isn't signed,' Leona pointed out.

'It will be,' Zafina stated certainly, 'as was agreed this morning at the meeting of the family heads. Sheikh Khalifa is dying. His loving son will deny him nothing. When we reach Rahman the signing will take place and the announcement will be made at Sheikh Khalifa's celebration banquet.'

He will deny him nothing… Of everything Zafina had said, those words were the only ones that held the poison. Still, Leona strove to reject them.

'You lie,' she said. 'No matter what this piece of paper says, and no matter what you imply. I know Hassan. I know my father-in-law, Sheikh Khalifa. Neither would even think of deceiving me this way.'

'You think not?' She sounded so sure, so confident. 'In the eyes of his country, Sheikh Hassan must prove his loyalty to them is stronger than his desire to pander to your western principles.'

More certain on having said it, Leona turned ice-cold eyes on the other woman. 'I will tell Hassan about this conversation. You do realise that?' she warned.

Zafina bowed her head in calm acquiescence. 'Face him,' she invited. 'Tell him what you know. He may continue to keep the truth from you for his father's sake. He may decide to confess all then fall on your mercy, hoping that you will still go to Rahman as his loyal first wife to help save his face. But mark my words, Sheikha,' she warned, 'my daughter will be Sheikh Hassan's wife before this month is out, and she will bear him the son that will make his life complete.'

Stepping forward, she retrieved her precious contract. 'I have no wish to see you humiliated,' she concluded as she turned towards the door. 'Indeed I give you this chance to save your face. Return to England. Divorce Hassan,' she advised. 'For, whether you do or not, he will marry my daughter, at which point I think we both know that your usefulness will be at an end.'

Leona let her go without giving her the satisfaction of a response, but as the door closed behind Zafina she began to shake. No, she told herself sternly, you will not let that woman's poison eat away at you. She's lying. Hassan would not be so deceitful or so manipulative. He loves you, for goodness' sake! Haven't you both just spent a whole afternoon re-avowing that love?

I will deny him nothing… Hassan's own words, exactly as spoken only days ago. Her stomach turned, sending her reeling for the bathroom. Yet she stopped herself, took a couple of deep controlling breaths and forced herself to think, to trust in her own instincts, to believe in Hassan!

He would not do it. Hands clenched into tense fists at her

sides, she repeated that. *He would not do it!* The woman is evil. She is ambitious. She cannot accept failure.

She used your own inadequacies against you. How dare you so much as consider anything she said as worthy of all of this anguish?

You promised to believe in him. How dare you let that promise falter because some awful woman wants you out of his life and her daughter in it?

A contract. What was the contract but a piece of paper with words written upon it? Anyone could draw up a contract; it was getting those involved to sign it that was the real test!

She would tell Hassan, let him deny it once and for all, then she could put all of this behind her and—

No she wouldn't. She changed her mind. She would not give that woman the satisfaction of causing more trouble between the families, which was what was sure to happen if Hassan did find out what Zafina had said.

Trust was the word. Trust she *would* give to him.

The door opened. She spun around to find Hassan standing there. Tall and dark, smooth and sleek, and so heart-achingly, heart-breakingly, precious to her.

'What is wrong?' He frowned. 'You look as pale as the carpet.'

'N-nothing,' she said. Then, because it was such an obvious lie, she admitted, 'H-headache, upset stomach…' Two tight fists unclenched, one hand going to cover her stomach the other her clammy forehead. 'Too much food tonight. T-too much water from my dip in the sea, maybe. I…'

He was striding towards her. Her man. Her beautiful, grim-faced man. He touched her cheek. 'You feel like ice.' He picked up her chafed wrist between gentle finger and thumb. 'Your pulse is racing like mad! You need the medic.' He spun towards the telephone. 'Get undressed. You are going to bed…'

'Oh…no, Hassan!' she cried out in protest. 'I will be okay in a couple of minutes! Please…' she pleaded as he picked up the telephone. 'Look!' she declared, as he glared at her from beneath frowning black brows. 'I'm feeling better already. I—took something a few minutes ago.' With a mammoth gathering together of self-control, she even managed to walk over to him without stumbling and took the receiver from his hand.

'No,' she repeated. 'I will not spoil everyone's enjoyment tonight. I've caused enough fuss today as it is.' And she would not give Zafina a moment's smug satisfaction. 'Walk me back along the deck.' Firmly she took his hand. 'All I need is some fresh air.'

He wasn't sure. But Leona ignored his expression and pulled him towards the door. Actually the walk did her more good than she had expected it to do. Just being with him, feeling his presence, was enough to help reaffirm her belief that he would never, ever, do anything so cruel as to lie about a second wife.

He's done it before, a small voice inside her head reminded her.

Oh, shut up! she told it. I don't want to listen. And she pasted a bright smile on her face, ready to show it to their waiting guests—and Zafina Al-Yasin—as she and Hassan stepped back into the salon.

Zafina wasn't there, which in a way was a relief and in another was a disappointment, because she so wanted to outface the evil witch. She had to make do with shining like a brilliant star for those left to witness it, and she wondered once or twice if she was going to burn out. And she was never more relieved when it became time to retire without causing suspicion that this was all just a dreadful front.

Raschid and Imran had collared Hassan. So she was free to droop the moment she hit the bedroom. Within ten minutes she was curled up in bed. Within another ten she was up again and giving in to what had been threatening to happen since Zafina's visit. Fortunately Hassan was not there to witness it. By the time he came to bed she had found escape in sleep at last, and he made no move to waken her, so morning arrived all too soon, and with it returned the nauseous sensation.

She got through the day by the skin of her teeth, and was pleasant to Zafina, who was not sure how to take that. She spent most of her morning with Evie and her children, taking comfort from the sheer normality of their simple needs and amusements. It was while she was playing with Hashim that the little boy inadvertently brushed against her breasts and she winced at their unexpectedly painful response.

Evie noticed the wince. 'You okay?' she enquired.

Her shrug was rueful. 'Actually, I feel a bit grotty,' she confessed. 'I ache in strange places after my fight with the fishing net yesterday, and I think the water I swallowed had bugs.'

'The same bugs that got you the day before that?' Evie quizzed.

'Okay,' she conceded. 'So I'm still stressed out.'

'Or something,' Evie murmured.

Leona's chin came up, 'What's that supposed to mean?' she demanded.

It was Evie's turn to offer a rueful shrug, then Raschid walked into the room and the conversation had to be shelved when he reminded them that lunch was being served.

After lunch came siesta time. Or, for those like Hassan and Raschid, time to hit the phones and deal with matters of state. Leona had never been so glad of the excuse to shut herself away in her room because she was really beginning to feel ill by then. Her head ached, her bones ached, her stomach was objecting to the small amount of food she had eaten for lunch.

Maybe it was a bug, she mused frowningly as she drew the curtains across the windows in an effort to diffuse the light that was hurting her eyes. Stripping off her top clothes, she then crawled into the bed.

Maybe she should have steered well clear of Evie's children just in case she had picked up something catching, she then added, and made herself a promise to mention it to Evie later just before she slipped into a heavy sleep.

She came awake only as a scarlet sunset seeped into the room. The last sunset before they reached Jeddah, she recalled with relief. And found the reminder gave her a fresh burst of energy that she took with her into the bathroom where she indulged in a long leisurely shower then took her time getting ready for dinner. She chose to wear a calf-length tunic made of spearmint-blue silk with a matching pair of slender-cut trousers.

Hassan arrived in the room with a frown and his mind clearly preoccupied.

'Hello stranger,' she said.

He smiled. It was an amazing smile, full of warmth, full of love—full of lazy suggestions as he began to run his eyes over her in that dark possessive way that said, Mine, most definitely mine. It was the Arab-male way. What the man did not bother to say with words he could make up for with expressive glances.

'No,' Leona said to this particular look. 'I am all dressed up and ready to play hostess, so keep your lecherous hands to yourself.'

'Of course, you do know that I could easily change your mind?' he posed confidently.

Jokes. Light jokes. Warm smiles and tender communication. Would this man she knew and loved so well look at her like this yet still hold such terrible secrets from her?

No, of course he would not, so stop thinking about it! 'Save it until later,' she advised, making a play of sliding the silk scarf over her hair.

His eyes darkened measurably. It was strange how she only now noticed how much he liked seeing her dressed Arabian style. Was it in his blood that he liked to see his woman modestly covered? Was it more than that? Did he actually prefer—?

No. She stopped herself again. Stop allowing that woman's poison to get to you.

'Wait for me,' he requested when she took a step towards the door. 'I need only five minutes to change, for I showered ten minutes ago, after allowing that over-energetic Samir talk me into a game of softball on the sun deck.'

'Who won?' she asked, changing direction to go and sit on the arm of one of the chairs to wait as requested.

'I did—by cheating,' he confessed.

'Did he know you cheated?'

'Of course,' Hassan replied. 'But he believes he is in my debt so he allowed me to get away with it.'

'You mean you played on his guilty conscience over my accident,' she accused.

He turned another slashing grin on her. It had the same force as an electric charge aimed directly at her chest. Heat flashed across her flesh in a blanket wave of sensual static. Followed by another wave of the same as she watched him strip off western shirt and shorts to reveal sleek brown flesh just made for fingers to stroke. By the time he had replaced the clothes with a white tunic he had earned himself a similar possessive glance to the one he had given her.

See, she told herself, you can't resist him in Arab dress. It has nothing to do with what runs in the blood. She even decided to tease him about it. 'If there is one thing I have learned to understand since knowing you, it is why men pre-fer women in dresses.'

'This is not a dress,' he objected.

Getting up, she went to stand in front of him and placed her palms flat against the wall of his chest to feel warm skin, tight and smooth, and irresistible to seeking hands that wanted to stroke a sensual pathway over muscled contours to his lean waist.

'I know what it is, my darling,' she murmured seductively. 'It is a sinful temptation, and therefore no wonder that you don't encourage physical contact between the sexes.'

His answering laugh was low and deep, very much the sound of a man who was aware of his own power to attract. 'Remind Samir of that, if you will,' he countered dryly. 'He is very lucky I have not beaten him to a pulp by now for the liberties he takes with my wife.'

But Samir, Leona discovered as soon as they entered the main salon, was more interested in extolling the liberties Hassan had taken with him. 'He cheats. He has no honour. He went to Eton, for goodness' sake, where they turn desert savages into gentlemen!'

'Oh…' Leona lifted her head to mock her husband. 'So that's what it is I love most about you.'

'The gentleman?'

'The savage,' she softly corrected.

He replied with a gentle cuff to her chin. Everyone laughed. Everyone was happy. Zafina tried very hard to hide her malicious glare.

They ate dinner beneath the stars that night. Leona was surprised to see a bed of ice holding several bottles of champagne waiting on a side table. Some of her guests drank alcohol; some of them did not. Wine was the favoured choice for those who did imbibe. But even when there had been cause to celebrate yesterday evening champagne had not been served.

'What's going on?' she asked Hassan as he saw her seated.

'Wait and see,' he replied frustratingly, and walked away to take his own seat at the other end of the table.

Ah, the last supper, she thought then, with a pinch of acid wit. And, believing she had her answer, she turned her attention to her meal, while Rafiq continued his opinions of men in high positions who could lower themselves to cheat.

The first spoonful of what was actually a delicious Arabian soup set Leona's stomach objecting. 'Never mind,' she said to soothe Samir's dramatically ruffled feathers as she quietly laid aside her spoon. 'Tomorrow you and I will race on the jet-skis and I promise that I, as an English gentlewoman, will not cheat.'

'Not on this trip, I am afraid,' Hassan himself inserted smoothly. 'All water sports are now stopped until we can replace the buoyancy aids with something more effective.'

Leona stared down the table at him. 'Just like that?' she protested. 'I have an unfortunate and one-in-a-million-chance accident and you put a stop on everyone else's fun?'

'You almost drowned. The life jacket did not do what it is designed to do. A million-to-one chance of it happening again makes the odds too great.'

'That is the voice of the master,' Samir noted.

'You heard it too, hmm?' Leona replied.

'Most indubitably,' Hassan agreed.

After that the conversation moved on to other things. Soup dishes were removed and replaced with a fish dish she didn't even attempt to taste. A richly sauced Arab dish followed, with a side bowl each of soft and fluffy steamed white rice.

The rice she thought she could just about manage to eat, Leona decided, listening intently to the story Imran Al-Mukhtar was telling her as she transferred a couple of spoonfuls of rice onto her plate then added a spoonful of sauce just for show.

One spoonful of soup, two forkfuls of rice. No fish. No attempt to even accept a sample of the thick honey pudding to conclude. Hassan watched it all, took grim note, glanced to one side to catch Evie's eye. She sent him a look that said that she had noticed too.

'The Sheikha Leona seems a little…pale,' Zafina Al-Yasin, sitting to one side of him, quietly put in. 'Is she not feeling quite herself?'

'You think so?' he returned with mild surprise. 'I think she looks exquisite. But then, I am smitten,' he allowed. 'It makes a difference as to how you perceive someone, don't you think?'

A steward came to stand at his side then, thankfully relieving him from continuing such a discussion.

With a nod of understanding he sent the steward hurrying over to the side table where he and his assistants began deftly uncorking the bottles of champagne. Picking up a spoon, he gave a couple of taps against a wine glass to capture everyone's attention.

'My apologies for interrupting your dinner,' he said, 'but in a few minutes our captain will sound the yacht's siren. As you can see, the stewards are in the process of setting a glass of champagne before each of you. It is not compulsory that you actually drink it,' he assured with a grin for those who never imbibed no matter what the occasion, 'but as a courtesy, in the time-honoured tradition of any sailing vessel. I would be most honoured if you would stand and join me by raising your glass in a toast. For we are about to cross the Tropic of Cancer…'

With the perfect timing of a man who was adept at such things, the siren gave three short sharp hoots at the same moment that Hassan rose to his feet. On a ripple of surprise everyone rose up also. Some drank, some didn't, but all raised their glasses. Then there was a mass exodus to the yacht's rail, where everyone stood gazing out into the inky dark Red Sea as if they expected to see some physical phenomenon like a thick painted line to mark this special place.

Of course there was none. It did not seem to matter. Moving to place his hands on the rail either side of his wife, Hassan bent to place his lips to her petal-smooth cheek.

'See anything?' he questioned teasingly.

'Oh, yes,' she replied. 'A signpost sticking out of the water. Did you miss it?'

His soft laugh was deep and soft and seductive. As she tilted back to look at him the back of her head met with his shoulder. She was smiling with her eyes. He wanted to drown in them. Kiss me, they were saying. An Arab did not kiss in front of guests, so a raised eyebrow ruefully refused the invitation. It was the witch in her that punished him for that refusal when one of her hands slid backwards and made a sensual sweep of one of his thighs.

Sensation spat hot pricks of awareness like needles deep into his flesh. She was right about the *dishdasha*, he conceded, it had to be one of the ancient reasons why his culture frowned upon close physical contact with the opposite sex whilst in the company of others.

'I will pay you back for that later,' he warned darkly.

'I am most seriously worried, my lord Sheikh,' she replied provokingly.

Then, in the way these things shifted, the private moment was broken when someone spoke to him. He straightened to answer Jibril Al-Mahmud who, since the meeting had spent every minute he could possibly snatch trying to squeeze himself back into Hassan's good graces. Leona took a sip at her champagne. That dreadful intruder, Samir, claimed the rest of her attention. He was, Hassan recognised, just a little infatuated with Leona, which offered another good reason why he would be happy when their cruise ended tomorrow.

Jibril's timid little wife came to join them. She smiled nervously at him and, because he felt rather sorry for her, Hassan sent her a pleasant smile back, then politely asked about her family. Raschid joined in. Evie and Imran went to join Leona and Samir. Abdul and Zafina were the last to join his own group but at least they did it, he acknowledged.

Tonight there was no splitting of the sexes. No lingering at the table for the men. They simply mingled, talked and lingered together. And, had it not been for one small but important detail, Hassan would have declared the evening— if not the whole cruise—a more than satisfactory success.

That small but important detail was Leona. Relaxed though she might appear, content though she might appear, he could see that the strain of the whole ordeal in general had begun to paint soft bruises around her eyes. He didn't like to see them there, did not like to notice that every so often the palm of her hand would go to rest against the flat of her stomach, as if to soothe away an inner distress.

Nor had he forgotten that she had barely eaten a morsel of food all day. He frowned down at his champagne glass, still brimming with its contents. Tomorrow they reached Jeddah. Tomorrow he would take her to visit a doctor, he decided grimly. If there was one rule you were taught never to ignore when you lived in a hot country, it was the rule about heeding any signs of illness. Maybe it was nothing.

Maybe it was all just down to stress. But maybe she had picked up something in the water when she fell in. Whatever—tomorrow he would make sure that they found out for definite.

It was a decision he found himself firmly repeating when they eventually retired to their stateroom and the first thing that Leona did was wilt.

'You are ill,' he said grimly.

'Just tired,' she insisted.

'Don't take me for a fool, Leona,' he ground back. 'You do not eat. You are clearly in some sort of discomfort. And you *look* ill.'

'All right.' She caved in. 'So I think I have developed a stomach bug. If we have time when we reach Jeddah to-morrow I will get something for it.'

'We will make time.'

'Fine.' She sighed.

He sighed. 'Here, let me help you...' She even looked too weary to undress herself.

So he did it for her—silently, soberly, a concentrated frown darkening his face. She smiled and kissed him. It really was too irresistible to hold the gesture in check. 'Don't turn into a minx just because I am indulging you,' he scolded, and parted the tunic, then let it slide to her feet.

'But I like it when you indulge me,' she told him, her eyes lowered to watch him reach for the front clasp holding the two smooth satin cups of her cream bra together. As the back of his knuckles brushed against the tips of her breasts she drew back with a sharp gasp.

'What?' he demanded.

'Sensitive.' She frowned. He frowned. They both glanced down to see the tight distension of her nipples standing pink and proud and wilfully erect. A small smug smile twitched at the corner of his mouth. Leona actually blushed.

'I'll finish the rest for myself,' she decided dryly.

'I think that would be wise,' Hassan grinned, and pulled

the *dishdasha* off over his head to show her why he had said that.

'I don't know.' She was almost embarrassed by how fiercely one responded to the closeness of the other. 'I'm supposed to be ill and tired and in need of much pampering.'

A set of warm brown fingers gently stroked the flush blooming in her cheek. 'I know of many ways to pamper,' he murmured sensually. 'Slow and gentle. Soft and sweet…'

His eyes glowed darkly with all of those promises; hers grew darker on the willingness to accept. The gap between them closed, warm flesh touched warm flesh, mouths came together on a kiss. Then he showed her. Deep into the night he showed her a hundred ways to pamper a woman until she eventually fell asleep in his arms and remained there until morning came to wake them up.

At breakfast she actually ate a half-slice of toast with marmalade and drank a full cup of very weak tea—hopefully without giving away the fact that it was a struggle not to give it all back up.

Little Hashim came to beg to be allowed to sit on her lap. Leona placed him there and together they enjoyed sharing the other half of her slice of toast, while Hassan looked on with a glaze across his eyes and Evie posed a sombre question at her husband, Raschid, with expressive eyes.

He got up and stepped around the table to lay a hand on Hassan's shoulder. The muscles beneath it were fraught with tension. 'I need a private word with you, Hassan,' he requested. 'If you have finished here?'

The same muscle flexed as Hassan pulled his mind back from where it had gone off to. 'Of course,' he said, and stood up. A moment later both men were walking away from the breakfast table towards the stairs which would take them down to the deck below and Hassan's private suite of offices.

Most watched them go. Many wondered why Sheikh Raschid felt it necessary to take Sheikh Hassan to one side. But none, friend nor foe—except for Evie, who kept her attention firmly fixed on the small baby girl in her arms—came even close to guessing what was about to be discussed.

By the time Raschid came to search his wife out she was back in their suite. She glanced anxiously up at him. Raschid lifted a rueful shoulder, 'Well, it is done,' he said. Though neither of them looked as if the statement pleased them in any way.

Well, it is done. That more or less said it. *Well it is done,* now held Hassan locked in a severe state of shock. He couldn't believe it. He wanted to believe it, but did not dare let himself because it changed everything: the view of his life; the view of his marriage.

He had to sit down. The edge of his desk was conveniently placed to receive his weight, and his eyes received the cover of a trembling hand. Beyond the closed door to his office his guests and the tail end of the cruise carried on regardless, but here in this room everything he knew and felt had come to a complete standstill.

He couldn't move. Now his legs had been relieved of his weight, they had lost the ability to take it back again. Inside he was shaking. Inside he did not know what to feel or what to think. For he had been here in this same situation before— many times—and had learned through experience that it was a place best avoided at all costs.

Hope—then dashed hopes. Pleasure—then pain. But this was different. This had been forced upon him by a source he had good reason to trust and not to doubt.

Doubt. Dear heaven, he was very intimate with the word doubt. Now, as he removed the hand from his eyes and stared out at the glistening waters he could see through the window, he found doubt being replaced by the kind of dancing visions he had never—ever—allowed himself to see before.

A knock sounded at the door, then it opened before he had a chance to hide his expression. Rafiq walked in, took one look at him and went rock solid still.

'What is it?' he demanded. 'Father?'

Hassan quickly shook his head. 'Come in and close the door,' he urged, then made an effort to pull himself together—just in case someone else decided to take him by surprise.

Leona.

Something inside him was suddenly threatening to explode. He didn't know what, but it scared the hell out of him. He wished Raschid had said nothing. He wished he could go back and replay the last half hour again, change it, lose it—

'Hassan…?' Rafiq prompted an explanation as to why he was witnessing his brother quietly falling apart.

He looked up, found himself staring into mirrors of his own dark eyes, and decided to test the ground—test those eyes to find out what Leona would see in his eyes if she walked in here right now.

'Evie—Raschid,' he forced out across a sand-dry throat. 'They think Leona might be pregnant. Evie recognises the signs…'

CHAPTER TEN

SILENCE fell. It was, Hassan recognised, a very deathly silence, for Rafiq was already showing a scepticism he dared not voice.

Understanding the feeling, Hassan released a hard sigh, then grimly pulled himself together. 'Get hold of our father,' he instructed. 'I need absolute assurance from him that I will not be bringing Leona back to a palace rife with rumour attached to her return.' From being hollowed by shock he was now as tight as a bowstring. 'If he has any doubts about this, I will place her in Raschid's safekeeping, for she must be protected at all cost from any more anguish or stress.'

'I don't think Leona will—'

'It is not and never has been anyone else's place to *think* anything about my wife!' The mere fact that he was lashing out at Rafiq showed how badly he was taking this. 'Other people's thinking has made our life miserable enough! Which is why I want you to speak to our father and not me,' he explained. 'I will have this conversation with no one else. Leona must be protected from ever hearing from anyone else that I am so much as suspecting this. If I am wrong then only I will grieve over what never was. If I am correct, then she has the right to learn of her condition for herself. I will not take this away from her!'

'So I am not even to tell our father,' Rafiq assumed from all of that.

'He and Leona communicate daily by e-mail,' Hasssan explained. 'The old man may be too puffed up with excitement to hold back from saying something to her.'

'In the state you are in, all of this planning may well be a waste of time,' Rafiq remarked with a pointed glance at his watch. 'In one hour we arrive in Jeddah. If you do not pull yourself together Leona will need only to look at your face to know that something catastrophic has taken place.'

Hassan knew it. Without warning he sank his face into his hands. 'This is crazy,' he muttered thickly.

'It is certainly most unexpected,' his brother agreed. 'And a little too soon for anyone, including the Al-Kadahs, to be making such confident judgements?' he posed cautiously.

Behind his hands Hassan's brain went still. Behind the hands it suddenly rushed ahead again, filling him with the kind of thoughts that made his blood run cold. For Rafiq was right: three weeks was not long enough—not to achieve what he was suggesting. As any man knew, it took only a moment to conceive a child. But which man—whose child?

On several hard curses he dragged his hand down. On several more he climbed to his feet then strode across the room to pull open the door that connected him with his aide.

'Faysal!' The man almost jumped out of his skin. 'Track down my father-in-law, wherever he is. I need to speak with him urgently.'

Slam. The door shut again. 'May Allah save me from the evil minds of others,' he grated.

'I do not follow you.' Rafiq frowned.

'Three weeks!' Hassan muttered. 'Three weeks ago Leona was sleeping in the same house as Ethan Hayes! It was one of the problems which forced me into bringing her to this yacht, if you recall...'

Leona didn't see Hassan until a few minutes before they were due to arrive in Jeddah. By then most of their guests were assembled on the shade deck taking refreshment while watching the yacht make the delicate manoeuvres required to bring such a large vessel safely into its reserved berth in the harbour.

In respect of Saudi Arabian custom everyone was wearing traditional Arab daywear, including little Hashim, who looked rather cute in his tiny white tunic and *gutrah*.

Hassan arrived dressed the same way; Rafiq was less than a step behind him. 'Hello, strangers.' Leona smiled at both of them. 'Where have you two been hiding yourselves all morning?'

'Working.' Rafiq smiled, but Hassan didn't even seem to hear her, and his gaze barely glanced across her face before he was turning to speak to Samir's father, Imran.

She frowned. He looked different—not pale, exactly, but under some kind of grim restraint. Then little Hashim demanded, 'Come and see,' and her attention was diverted. After that she had no time to think of anything but the formalities involved in bidding farewell to everyone.

A fleet of limousines stood in line along the concrete jetty waiting to speed everyone off to their various destinations. Accepting thanks and saying goodbye took over an hour. One by one the cars pulled up and took people away in a steady rota. Sheikh Abdul and Zafina first—relieved, Leona suspected, to be getting away from a trip that had not been a pleasant one for them, though their farewells were polite enough.

Sheikh Imran and Samir were the next to leave. Then she turned to smile at Sheikh Jibril and his wife, Medina, who made very anxious weight of their farewell, reminding Hassan several times that he had complete loyalty. In Jibril's case money talked much louder than power. He had no desire to scrape his deep pockets to pay Sheikh Raschid for the privilege of sending his oil across his land.

Raschid and his family were the last ones to leave. As with everyone else it would be a brief parting, because they would come together again next week, when they attended Sheikh Kalifa's anniversary celebration. Only this time the children would be staying at home with their nurse. So Leona's goodbyes to them were tinged with a genuine regret, especially for Hashim, who had become her little friend during their cruise. So, while she was promising to come and visit with him soon, she missed the rather sober exchanges between the others.

Eventually they left. Their car sped away. Rafiq excused himself to go and seek out Faysal, and Hassan said he had yet to thank his captain and walked away leaving her standing there, alone by the rail, feeling just a little bit rejected by the brevity with which he had treated her.

Something was wrong, she was sure, though she had no idea exactly what it could be. And, knowing him as well as she did, she didn't expect to find out until he felt ready to tell her. So with a shrug and a sigh she went off to follow Hassan's lead and thank the rest of the staff for taking care of everyone so well. By the time they came together again there was only time left to make the dash to the airport if they wanted to reach Rahman before nightfall.

Rafiq and Faysal travelled with them, which gave Hassan the excuse—and Leona was sure it *was* an excuse—to keep conversation light and neutral. A Lear jet bearing the gold Al-Qadim insignia waited on the runway to fly them over Saudi Arabia and into Rahman. The Al-Qadim oasis had its own private runway. A four-wheel drive waited to transport them to the palace whose ancient sandstone walls burned red against a dying sun.

Home, Leona thought, and felt a lump form in her throat because this was home to her. London…England—both had stopped being that a long time ago.

They swept through the gates and up to the front entrance. Hassan helped her to alight. As she walked inside she found herself flanked by two proud males again and wanted to lift her head and say something teasing about *abayas*, but the mood didn't allow for it somehow.

'My father wishes to see us straight away.' Hassan unwittingly explained the sombre mood. 'Please try not to show your shock at how much he has deteriorated since you were last here.'

'Of course,' she replied, oddly hurt that he felt he needed to say that. Then she took the hurt back when she saw the old sheikh reclining against a mound of pillows on his favourite divan.

His sons strode forward; she held back a little to allow them the space to greet him as they always did, with the old sheikh holding out both hands and both hands being taken, one by each son. In all the years she had known Sheikh Kalifa she had never seen him treat his two sons less than equal. They greeted each other; they talked in low-toned Arabic. They touched, they loved. It was an honour and a privilege to be allowed to witness it. When the old sheikh decided to acknowledge her presence he did so with a spice that told her that the old spirit was still very much alive inside his wasted frame.

'So, what do you think of my two warriors, huh?' he asked. 'They snatch you back with style and panache. A worthy woman cannot but be impressed.'

'Impressed by their arrogance, their cheek, and their disregard for my safety,' Leona responded, coming forward now that he had in effect given her permission to do so. 'I almost drowned—twice—and was tossed down a set of stairs. And you dare to be proud of them.'

No one bothered to accuse her of gross exaggeration, because he laughed, loving it, wishing he could have been there to join in. Reclaiming his hands, he waved his sons away and offered those long bony fingers to Leona.

'Come and greet me properly,' he commanded her. 'And you two can leave us. My daughter-in-law and I have things to discuss.'

There was a pause, a distinct hesitation in which Hassan looked ready to argue the point. The old man looked up at him and his son looked down; a battle of the eyes commenced that made Leona frown as a strange kind of tension began to sizzle in the air. Then Hassan conceded by offering a brief, grim nod and left, with Rafiq making the situation feel even stranger when, as he left with him, he placed a hand on Hassan's shoulder as if to reassure him that it would be okay.

'What was all that about?' she enquired as she reached down to brush a kiss on her father-in-law's hollowed cheek.

'He worries about you,' the old sheikh answered.

'Or he worries about you,' she returned.

He knew what she was referring to and flicked it away with a sigh and a wave of a hand. 'I am dying,' he stated bluntly. 'Hassan knows this—they both do. Neither likes knowing they can do nothing to stop it from happening.'

'But you are resigned?' Leona said gently.

'Yes. Come—sit down here, in your chair.' Discussion over, he indicated the low cushion-stuffed chair she had pulled up beside his divan years ago; it had remained there ever since. 'Now, tell me,' he said as soon as she was settled, 'have you come back here because Hassan bullied you into doing so, or because you still love him?'

'Can it be both?' she quizzed him.

'He needs you.'

'Rahman doesn't.'

'Ah,' he scathed, 'that stupid man, Abdul, thought he could force our hand and soon learned that he could not.'

'So it was Sheikh Abdul who plotted to take me,' Leona murmured ruefully.

Eyes that were once a rich dark brown but were now only pale shadows sharpened. 'He did not tell you,' he surmised on an impatient sigh. 'I am a fool for thinking he would.'

'Maybe that is why he didn't want to leave me alone with you,' Leona smilingly replied. 'Actually, I had already guessed it,' she then admitted, adding quietly, 'I know all about Nadira, you see.'

The name had a disturbing effect on Sheikh Khalifa: he shifted uncomfortably, pulled himself up and reached out to touch her cheek. 'Rahman needs my son and my son needs you. Whatever has to happen in the future I need to know that you will always be here supporting him when I can no longer do so.'

Strange words, fierce, dark, compelling words that sealed her inside a coating of ice. What was he saying? What did he mean? Was he telling her that Nadira was still Hassan's only real option if he wanted to continue in his father's footsteps?

But before she could ask him to elaborate, as after most brief bursts of energy, Sheikh Khalifa suddenly lay back exhausted against the cushions and, without really thinking about it, Leona slipped back into her old routine. She picked up the book lying face down on the table beside him and began reading out loud to him.

But her mind was elsewhere. Her mind was filling up with contracts and Hassan's method of feeding her information on a need-to-know only basis. She saw him as he had been that same morning, relaxed, at peace with both her and himself. Then Raschid had begged a private word. When he'd eventually reappeared later it had been as if he had changed into a different man—a tense, preoccupied and distant man.

A man who avoided eye contact, as if he had something to hide...

The old sheikh was asleep. Leona put down the book.

Doubts; she hated to feel the doubts return. It was no use, she told herself, she was going to have to tackle Hassan about what Zafina had said to her. Once he had denied everything she could put the whole stupid thing away, never to be dredged up again.

And if he didn't deny it? she asked herself as she left the old sheikh's room to go in search of the younger one. The coating of ice turned itself into a heavy cloak that weighed down her footsteps as she walked in between pale blue walls on a cool, polished sandstone flooring.

She didn't want to do this, she accepted as she trod the wide winding staircase onto the landing where pale blue walls changed to pale beige and the floor became a pale blue marble.

She didn't want to reveal that she could doubt his word, she thought dully as she passed between doors made of thick cedar fitted tightly into wide Arabian archways, the very last one of which led through to Hassan's private suite of offices.

Her head began to ache; her throat suddenly felt strange:

hot and tight. She was about five yards away when the door suddenly opened and Hassan himself stepped out. Slender white tunic, flowing blue *thobe*, no covering on his raven-dark head. He saw her and stopped, almost instantly his expression altered from the frowningly preoccupied to... nothing.

It was like having a door slammed in her face. Her doubts surged upwards along with her blood pressure; she could feel her pulse throbbing in her ears. A prickly kind of heat engulfed her whole body—and the next thing that she knew, she was lying on the pale blue marble floor and Hassan was kneeling beside her.

'What happened?' he rasped as her eyes fluttered open.

She couldn't answer, didn't want to answer. She closed her eyes again. His curse wafted across her cheeks. One of his hands came to cover her clammy forehead, the other took a light grasp of her wrist then he was grimly sliding his arms beneath her shoulders and knees and coming to his feet.

'Ouch,' she said as her breasts brushed his breastbone.

Hassan froze. She didn't notice because from absolutely nowhere she burst into tears! What was the matter with her? she wondered wretchedly. She felt sick, she felt dizzy, she hurt in places she had never hurt before! From another place she had never known existed inside her, one of her clenched fists aimed an accusing blow at his shoulder.

Expecting him to demand what he had done to deserve it, she was thrown into further confusion when all he did was release a strained groan from deep in his throat, then began striding back the way from which she had come. A door opened and closed behind them. Lifting her head from his shoulder, she recognised their old suite of rooms.

Laying her on the bed, he came to lean over her. 'What did my father say to you?' he demanded. 'I knew I should not have left you both alone! Did he say you should not have come back, is that it?'

Her eyes flew open, tear-drenched and sparkling. 'Is that what he thinks?'

'Yes—no!' His sigh was driven by demons. But what demons—? The demons of lies? 'In case you did not notice, he does not think so clearly any more,' he said tightly.

'Sheikh Abdul was behind the plot to abduct me; there is nothing unclear about that, as far as I can see.'

'I knew it was a mistake.' Hassan sighed, and sat down beside her.

He looked tired and fed up and she wanted to hit him again. 'You lied to me again,' she accused him.

'By omission,' he agreed. 'And Abdul's involvement cannot be proved,' he added. 'Only by hearsay which is not enough to risk a war between families.'

'And you've always got the ready-typed contract involving Nadira if things really do get out of hand...'

This time she saw the freeze overtake him. This time she got the answer she had been desperately trying to avoid. Sitting up, Leona ignored the way her head spun dizzily. Drawing up her knees, she reached down to ease the straps of her sandals off the backs of her heels, then tossed them to the floor.

'He told you about that also?' Hassan asked hoarsely.

She shook her head. 'Zafina did.'

'When?'

'Does it really matter when?' she derided. 'It exists. I saw it. You felt fit not to warn me about it. What do you think that tells me about what is really going on around here?'

'It means nothing,' he claimed. 'It is just a meaningless piece of paper containing words with no power unless several people place their signatures against it.'

'But you have a copy.'

He didn't answer.

'You had it in your possession even before you came to Spain to get me,' she stated, because she knew it was the truth even though no one had actually told her so. 'What was it—firm back-up in case Raschid failed to bail you out of trouble? Or does it still carry a lot of weight around with it?'

'You could try trusting me,' he answered.

'And you, my lord sheikh, should have tried trusting me, then maybe it would not be the big problem it is.' With that, she climbed off the bed and began walking away.

'Where are you going?' He sighed out heavily. 'Come back here. We need to—'

The cold way she turned to look at him stopped the words; the way she had one hand held to her forehead and the other to her stomach paled his face. 'I am going to the bathroom to be sick,' she informed him. 'Then I am going to crawl into that bed and go to sleep. I would appreciate it if you were not still here when I get to do that.'

And that, Hassan supposed, had told him. He watched the bathroom door close behind her retreating figure.

He got up and strode over to the window beyond which an ink dark evening obliterated everything beyond the subtle lighting of the palace walls.

So where do we go from here? he asked himself. When Zafina Al-Yasin had picked her weapon, she'd picked it well. For Hassan could think of nothing more likely to shatter Leona's belief in his sincerity than a document already drawn up and ready to be brought into use should it become necessary. She would not now believe that he had agreed to the drawing up of such a document merely to buy him time. Why should she when he had refrained from telling her so openly and honestly before she'd found out by other means?

Sighing, he turned to leave the room. It was simpler to leave her alone for now. He could say nothing that was going to change anything, because he had another problem looming, he realised, One bigger and more potentially damaging than all that had tried to damage his marriage before.

He had a contract bearing his agreement to take a second wife. He had a wife whom he suspected might be carrying his first child. Leona was never going to believe that the former was not an insurance policy to protect him against the failure of the latter.

'Faysal,' he said as he stepped into his aide's office, which guarded the entrance to his own, 'get Rafiq for me, if you please…'

'You look pale like a ghost,' the old sheikh remarked.

'I'm fine,' Leona assured him.

'They tell me you fainted the other day.'

'I still had my sea legs on,' Leona explained. 'And how did you find out about it?' she challenged, because as far as she knew no one but herself and Hassan had been there at the time!

'My palace walls are equipped with a thousand eyes.' He smiled. 'So I also know that when he is not with me my son walks around wearing the face of a man whose father is already dead.'

'He is a busy man doing busy, important things,' Leona said with a bite that really should have been resisted.

'He also has a wife who sleeps in one place while he sleeps in another.'

Getting in practice, Leona thought nastily. 'Do you want to finish this chapter or not?' she asked.

'I would prefer you to confide in me,' the old sheikh murmured gently. 'You used to do so all the time, before I became too sick to be of any use to anyone…'

A blatant plucking of her heartstrings though it was, Leona could see the concern in his eyes. On a sigh, she laid the book aside, got up to go and sit down beside him and picked up one of his cool, dry, skeletal hands to press a gentle kiss to it.

'Don't fret so, old man,' she pleaded gently. 'You know I will look after your two sons for you. I have promised, haven't I?'

'But you are unhappy. Do you think this does not fret me?'

'I—struggle with the reasons why I am here,' she explained, because she wasn't going to lie. It wasn't fair to lie to him. 'You know the problems. They are not going to go away just because Hassan wants them to.'

'My son wants you above all things, daughter of Victor Frayne,' he said, using the Arab way of referring to her, because by their laws a woman kept her father's name after marriage. 'Don't make him choose to prove this to you...'

CHAPTER ELEVEN

DON'T make him choose... The next day, those words played inside Leona's head like a mantra, because she had just begun to realise that Hassan might not be forced to choose anything.

Sickness in the morning, sickness in the evening, a certain tenderness in her breasts and other changes in her body that she could no longer ignore were trying to tell her something she was not sure she wanted to know.

Pregnant. She could be pregnant. She *might* be pregnant. She absolutely refused to say that she was *most definitely* pregnant. How could she be sure, when her periods had never been anything but sporadic at best? Plus it had to be too soon to tell. It had to be. She was just wishing on rainbows—wasn't she?

A month. She had been back in Hassan's life for a tiny month—and not even a full month! Women just didn't know that quickly if they had conceived, did they? She didn't know. At this precise moment she didn't know anything. Her brain was blank, her emotions shot and she was fighting an ever-growing battle with excitement that was threatening to turn her into a puff of smoke!

It was this morning that had really set her suspicions soaring, when she'd climbed out of bed feeling sick and dizzy before her feet had managed to touch the floor. Then, in the shower, she'd seen the changes in her breasts, a new fullness, darkening circles forming round their tips. She'd *felt* different too—inside, where it was impossible to say how she felt different, only that she did.

Instinct. What did she know about the female instinct in such situations?

Doubt. She had to doubt her own conclusions because the specialists had given her so little hope of it ever happening for them.

But even her skin felt different, her hair, the strange, secret glint she kept on catching in her own eyes whenever she looked in a mirror. She'd stopped looking in the mirror. It was easier not to look than look and then see, then dare—*dare* to hope.

I want Hassan, she thought on a sudden rocketing rise of anxiety.

I don't want Hassan! she then changed her mind. Because if he saw her like this he would know something really drastic was worrying her and she couldn't tell him—didn't dare tell him, raise his hopes, until she was absolutely sure for herself.

She needed one of those testing kits, she realised. But, if such a thing was obtainable, where could she get one from without alerting half of Rahman? There was not a chemist's in the country she could walk into and buy such an obvious thing without setting the jungle drums banging from oasis to oasis and back again.

But I need one. I *need* one! she thought agitatedly.

Ring Hassan, that tiny voice inside her head persisted. Tell him your suspicions, get him to bring a pregnancy testing kit home with him.

Oh, yes, she mocked that idea. I can just see Sheikh Hassan Al-Qadim walking into a chemist's and buying one of those!

Rafiq, then. No, *not* Rafiq! she all but shouted at herself. Oh, why could there not be some more women in this wretched house of Al-Qadim? Why do I have to be surrounded by men?

Maids. There were dozens of maids she could call upon— all of whom would be just as proficient at belting out the message across the whole state.

As if she'd conjured her up a knock sounded on the door and one of the maids walked into the room. She was carrying a dress that Leona had ordered to be delivered from one of her favourite couturier's in the city.

'It is very beautiful, my lady,' the maid said shyly.

And very red, Leona thought frowningly. What in heaven's name had made her choose to buy red? Made by a local designer to a traditional Arabian design, the dress was silk, had matching trousers and *thobe*, and shimmered with beautifully embroidered golden threads. And she never, ever wore red!

'The sheikha will shine above all things tomorrow night,' the maid approved.

Tomorrow night, Leona repeated with a sinking heart as the maid carried the dress into her dressing room. For tomorrow night was *the* night of Sheikh Kalifa's anniversary celebration, which meant she had a hundred guests to play hostess to when really all she wanted to do was—

Oh, she thought suddenly, where is my head? And she turned to walk quickly across the room towards the telephone which sat beside the bed.

Pregnant.

Her feet pulled to a stop. Her stomach twisted itself into a knot then sprang free again, catching at her breath. It was a desperate sensation. Desperate with hope and with fear and a thousand other things that—

The maid appeared again, looked at her oddly because she was standing here in the middle of the room, emulating a statue. 'Thank you, Leila,' she managed to say.

As soon as the door closed behind the maid she finished her journey to the telephone, picked up her address book, flicked through its pages with trembling fingers, then stabbed in a set of numbers that would connect her with Evie Al-Kadah in Behran.

Hassan was fed up. He was five hours away from home, on his way back from Sheikh Abdul's summer palace, having just enjoyed a very uncomfortable meeting in which a few home truths had been aired. He should be feeling happy, for the meeting had gone very much his way, and in his possession he now had the sheikh's copy of one ill-judged contract and the satisfaction of knowing the man and his wife now understood the error of their ways.

But it had required a five-hour drive out to mountains of Rahman to win this sense of grim satisfaction, which meant they now had to make the same journey back again. And Rafiq might feel *he* needed the physical exercise of negotiating the tough and challenging terrain but, quite frankly, so did he. He felt tense and restless, impatient to get back to Leona now that he could face her with an easy conscience.

So the flat tire they suffered a few minutes later was most unwelcome. By the time they had battled in soft sand on a rocky incline to jack the car up and secure it so they could change the wheel time was getting on, and the sun was beginning to set. Then, only a half-mile further into their journey, they became stuck in deep soft sand. And he couldn't even blame Rafiq for this second inconvenience because he had taken over the driving for himself. Proficient though they were at getting themselves out of such difficulties, time was lost, then more time when they were hit by a sandstorm that forced them to stop and wait until it had blown past.

Consequently, it was very late when they drove through the gates of the palace. By the time he had washed the sand from his body before letting himself quietly into the bedroom he found Leona fast asleep.

Did he wake her or did he go away? he pondered as he stood looking down on her, lying there on her side, with her glorious hair spilling out behind her and a hand resting on the pillow where his head should be.

She murmured something, maybe because she sensed he was there, and the temptation to just throw caution to the wind, slide into the bed and awaken her so he could confide his suspicions then discover whether she felt he was making any sense almost got the better of him.

Then reality returned, for this was not the time for such an emotive discussion. It could backfire on him and deeply hurt her. And tomorrow was a day packed with strife enough for both of them, without him adding to it with what could be merely a foolish dream.

Anyway, he had some damage limitation to perform, preferably before this new development came into the open—just in case.

So, instead of waking her, he turned away, unaware that behind him her eyes had opened to watch him leave. The urge to call him back tugged at her vocal cords. The need to scramble out of the bed and go after him to confide her suspicions stretched nerve ends in every muscle she possessed.

But, no, it would not be fair to offer him hope where there might be none. Better to wait one more day until she knew for sure one way or another, she convinced herself.

So the door between their two rooms closed him away from her—just as it had closed him away before, when he had decided it was better to sleep elsewhere than risk another argument with her.

Maybe he was right. Maybe the common sense thing to do was stay out of each other's way, because they certainly didn't function well together unless they were in bed!

They had a battleground, not a marriage, she decided, and on that profound thought she turned her back on that wretched closed door and refused to look back at it.

The next day continued in much the same fashion. He avoided her. She avoided him. They circulated the palace in opposing directions like a pair of satellites designed never to cross paths. By six o'clock Leona was in her room preparing for the evening ahead. By seven she was as ready as she supposed she ever would be, having changed her mind about what to wear a hundred times before finally deciding to wear the red outfit.

When Hassan stepped into the room a few minutes later he took her breath away. Tall, lean and not yet having covered his silky dark hair, he was wearing a midnight blue long tunic with a standing collar braided in gold. At his waist a wide sash of gold silk gave his body shape and stature, and the jewel encrusted shaft belonging to the ceremonial scabbard he had tucked into his waistband said it all.

Arrogance personified. A prince among men. First among equals did not come into it for her because for her he was it—the one—her only one. As if to confirm that thought her belly gave a skittering flutter as if to say, And me, don't forget me.

Too soon for that, too silly to think it, she scolded herself as she watched him pause to look at her. As always those dark eyes made their possessive pass over her. As always they liked what they saw.

'Beautiful,' he murmured.

Tell me about it, she wanted to say, but she couldn't, didn't dare say anything in case the wrong thing popped anxiously out.

So the twist his mouth gave said he had misread her silence. 'Forgiveness, my darling, is merely one sweet smile away,' he drawled as he walked towards her.

'But you have nothing to forgive me for!' she protested, glad now to use her voice.

'Throwing me out of your bed does not require forgiveness?' An eyebrow arched, the outfit, the coming occasion, turning the human being into a pretentious monster that made her toes curl inside her strappy gold shoes. With life, that was what they curled with. Life.

I love this man to absolute pieces. 'You left voluntarily,' she told him. 'In what I think you would describe as a sulk.'

'Men do not sulk.'

But you are not just any man, she wanted to say, but the comment would puff up his ego, so she settled for, 'What do they do, then?'

'Withdraw from a fight they have no hope of winning.' He smiled. Then on a complete change of subject, he said, 'Here, a peace offering.' And he held out a flat package wrapped in black silk and tied up with narrow red ribbon.

Expecting the peace offering to be jewellery, the moment

she took possession of the package she knew it was too light. So…what? she asked herself, then felt her heart suddenly drop to her slender ankles as a terrible suspicion slid snake-like into her head.

No, she denied it. Evie just would not break such a precious confidence. 'What is it?' she asked warily.

'Open it and see.'

Trembling fingers did as he bade her, fumbling with the ribbon and then with the square of black silk. Inside it was a flat gold box, the kind that could be bought at any gift shop, nothing at all like she had let herself wonder, and nothing particularly threatening about it, but still she felt her breath snag in her chest as she lifted the lid and looked inside.

After that came the frown while she tried to work out why Hassan was giving her a box full of torn scraps of white paper. Then she turned the top one over, recognised the insignia embossed upon it and finally realised what it was.

'You know what they are?' he asked her quietly.

'Yes.' She swallowed.

'All three copies of the contract are now in your possession,' he went on to explain anyway. 'All evidence that they were ever composed wiped clean from Faysal's computer hard disk. There, it is done. Now we can be friends again.' Without giving her a chance to think he took the gift and its packaging back from her and tossed it onto the bed.

'But it doesn't wipe clean the fact that it was written in the first place,' she pointed out. 'And nor does it mean it can't be typed up again in five short minutes if it was required to be done.'

'You have said it for yourself,' Hassan answered. 'I must require it. I do not require it. I give you these copies for ceremonial purposes, only to *show* you that I do not require it. Subject over, Leona,' he grimly concluded, 'for I will waste no more of my time on something that had only ever been meant as a diversion tactic to buy me time while I decided what to do about Sheikh Abdul and his ambitious plans.'

'You expect me to believe all of that, don't you?'

'Yes.' It was a coldly unequivocal yes.

She lifted her chin. For the first time in days they actually made eye contact. And it was only as it happened that she finally began to realise after all of these years *why* they avoided doing it when there was dissension between them. Eye contact wiped out everything but the truth. The *love* truth. The *need* truth. The absolute and utter *total* truth. I love him; he loves me. Who or what else could ever really come between that?

'I think I'm pregnant,' she whispered.

It almost dropped him like a piece of crumbling stone at her feet. She saw the shock; she saw the following pallor. She watched his eyes close and feared for a moment that *he* was actually going to faint.

For days he had been waiting for this moment, Hassan was thinking. He had yearned for it, had begged and had prayed for it. Yet, when it came, not only had he not been ready, the frightened little remark had virtually knocked him off his feet!

'I could kill you for this,' he ground out hoarsely. 'Why here? Why now, when in ten short minutes we are expected downstairs to greet a hundred guests?'

His response was clearly not the one she had been expecting. Her eyes began to glaze, her mouth to tremble. 'You don't like it,' she quavered.

'Give me strength.' He groaned. 'You stupid, unpredictable, aggravating female. Of course I like it! But look at me! I am now a white-faced trembling mess!'

'You just gave me something I really needed. I wanted to give you something back that you needed,' she explained.

'Ten minutes before I face the upper echelons of Arabian society?'

'Well, thanks for being concerned about how I am feeling!' she flashed back at him.

She was right. 'You've just knocked me for six,' he breathed unsteadily.

'And I might be wrong, so don't start going off the deep end about it!' she snapped, and went to turn away.

Oh, Allah, help him, what was he doing here? With shaking hands he took hold of her by her silk-swathed shoulders and pulled her against him. She was trembling too. And she *felt* different, slender and frail and oh, so precious.

He kissed her— What else did a man do when he was so blown away by everything about her?

'I should not have dropped it on you like this,' she murmured repentantly a few seconds later.

'Yes, you should,' he argued. 'How else?'

'It might come to nothing.' Anxiety was playing havoc with her beautiful eyes.

'We will deal with the something or the nothing together.'

'I am afraid of the nothing,' she confessed to him. 'I am afraid I might never get the chance to feel like this again.'

'I love you,' he said huskily. 'Can that not be enough?'

'For you?' She threw the question back at him, clinging to his eyes like a vulnerable child.

'We know how I feel, Leona,' he said ruefully. 'In fact, the whole of Rahman knows how I feel about you. But we hardly ever discuss how you feel about the situation I place you in here.'

'I just don't want you to have to keep defending my place in your life,' she told him. 'I hate it.'

Hassan thought about the damage-control exercise he had already set into motion, and wished he knew how to answer that. 'I like defending you.' His words seemed to say it all for him.

'You won't tell anyone tonight, will you?' she flashed up at him suddenly. 'You will keep this our secret until we know for sure.'

'Do you really think I am that manipulative?' He was shocked, then uncomfortable, because he realised that she knew him better than he knew himself. 'Tomorrow we will bring in a doctor,' he decided, looking for an escape from his own manipulative thoughts.

But Leona shook her head. 'It would be all over Rahman in five minutes if we did that. Look what happened when I went to see him to find out why I couldn't conceive?'

'But we have to know—'

'Evie is bringing me a pregnancy testing kit with her,' she told him, too busy trying to smooth some semblance of calmness into herself to notice how still he had gone. 'I rang her and explained. At least I can trust her not to say anything to anyone.'

'What did she say?' Hassan enquired carefully.

'She said I should make sure I tell you. Which I've done.' She turned a wry smile on him. 'Now I wish that I hadn't because, looking at you, I have a horrible feeling you are going to give the game away the moment anyone looks at you.'

Confess all, he told himself. Tell her before the Al-Kadahs tell her that you already suspected all of this, days ago. A knock at the door was a thankful diversion. Going to open it, he found Rafiq standing there dressed very much like himself—only he was wearing his *gutrah*.

'Our guests are arriving,' he informed him. 'You and Leona should be downstairs.'

Guests. Dear heaven. His life was in crisis and he must go downstairs and be polite to people. 'We will be five minutes only.'

'You are all right?' Rafiq frowned at him.

No, I am slowly sinking beneath my own plots and counter-plots. 'Five minutes,' he repeated, and closed the door again.

Leona was standing by a mirror, about to fix her lipstick with a set of very unsteady fingers. The urge to go over there and stop her so that he could kiss her almost got the better of him. But one kiss would most definitely lead to another and another. In fact he wanted to be very primitive and drag her off by her beautiful hair to his lair and smother her in kisses. So instead he stepped back into the other room and came back a moment later wearing white silk on his head, held by triple gold thongs, to find that Leona had also covered her hair with a gold-spangled scarf of red silk.

The red should have clashed with her hair but it didn't. It merely toned with the sensual colour on her lips. She lifted her eyes to look at him. He looked back at her. A different man, a different woman. It was amazing what a piece of silk laid to the head could do for both of them, because neither was now showing signs of what was really going on inside them.

His smile, therefore, was rueful. 'Showtime,' he said.

And showtime it was. As on the yacht, but on a grander scale, they welcomed heads of state from all over Arabia, diplomats from further afield. Some brought their wives, sons and even their daughters, and some came alone. Some women were veiled; all were dressed in the exotic jewelled colours favoured by Arabian women.

Everyone was polite, gracious, and concerned about Sheikh Khalifa's well-being. He had not yet put in an appearance, though he had every intention of doing so eventually. This was his night. He had in fact planned it as much as he could from his sick bed. Today his doctor had insisted he be sedated for most of the day to conserve his energy. But he had looked bright-eyed and excited when Leona had popped in to see him just before she had gone to get ready.

'Rafiq should be doing this with us,' Leona said to Hassan when she realised that his brother was nowhere to be seen.

'He has other duties,' he replied, then turned his attention to the next person to arrive at the doors to the great hall. A great hall that was slowly filling with people.

Sheikh Abdul arrived without his wife, Zafina, which seemed a significant omission to Leona. He was subdued but polite to her, which was all she could really expect from him, she supposed. They greeted Sheikh Jibril and his wife, Medina, Sheikh Imran, and of course Samir.

When Sheikh Raschid Al-Kadah and his wife, Evie, ar-

rived, there were some knowing glances exchanged that
made Leona want to blush. But the real blushing happened
every time Hassan glanced at her and his eyes held the burning darkness of their secret.

'Don't,' she whispered, looking quickly away from him.

'I cannot help it,' he replied.

'Well, try.' A sudden disturbance by the door gave her
someone new to divert her attention, only to have her heart
stop in complete surprise.

Two men dressed in black western dinner suits, white
shirts and bow ties. She flicked her eyes from one smiling
male face to the other, then on a small shriek of delight
launched herself into the arms of her father.

Tall, lean and in very good shape for his fifty-five years,
Victor Frayne caught his daughter to him and accepted her
ecstatic kisses to his face. 'What are you doing here? Why
didn't you tell me? Ethan—' One of her hands reached out
to catch one of his. 'I can't believe this! I only spoke to you
this morning. I thought you were in San Estéban!'

'No, the Marriott, here.' Her father grinned at her. 'Thank
your husband for the surprise.'

Hassan. She turned, a hand each clinging to her two surprises. 'I love you,' she said impulsively.

'She desires to make me blush,' Hassan remarked, and
stepped forward, took his wife by her waist, then offered his
hand to his father-in-law and to Ethan Hayes. 'Glad you
could make it,' he said.

'Happy to be here,' Ethan replied with only a touch of
dryness to his tone to imply that there was more to this invitation than met the eye.

Leona was just too excited to notice. Too wrapped up in
her surprise to notice the ripple of awareness that went
through those people who had dared to believe rumours
about her relationship with her father's business partner.
Then, with the attention to fine detail which was Hassan's
forte, another diversion suddenly appeared.

People stopped talking, silence reigned as Rafiq arrived,

pushing a wheelchair bearing Sheikh Khalifa ben Jusef Al-Qadim.

He looked thin and frail against the height and breadth of his youngest son. A wasted shadow of his former self. But his eyes were bright, his mouth smiling, and in the frozen stasis that followed his arrival, brought on by everyone's shock at how ill he actually looked, he was prepared and responded. 'Welcome…welcome everyone,' he greeted. 'Please, do not continue to look as if you are attending my funeral, for I assure you I am here to enjoy myself.'

After that everyone made themselves relax again. Some who knew him well even grinned. As Rafiq wheeled him towards the other end of the room the old sheikh missed no one in reach of his acknowledgement. Not even Leona's father, whom he had only met once or twice. 'Victor,' he greeted him. 'I have stolen your daughter. She is now my most precious daughter. I apologise to you, but I am not sorry, you understand?'

'I think we can share her,' Victor Frayne allowed graciously.

'And…ah…' he turned his attention to Ethan '…Mr Hayes, it is my great pleasure to meet Leona's very good friend.' He had the floor, as it should be. So no one could miss the messages being broadcast here. Even Leona began to notice that something was going on beneath the surface here. 'Victor…Mr Hayes…come and see me tomorrow. I have a project I believe will be of great interest to you… Ah, Rafiq, take me forward, for I can see Sheikh Raschid…'

He progressed down the hall like that. As Leona watched, she gently slipped her arm around Hassan's waist. She could feel the emotion pulsing inside him. For this was probably going to be the old Sheikhs final formal duty.

But nothing, nothing prepared her for the power of feeling that swept over everyone as Rafiq and his father reached the other end of the hall where Sheikh Khalifa's favourite divan had been placed upon a raised dais, ready for him to enjoy the party in reasonable comfort.

Rafiq bent and lifted his father into his arms and carried the frail old man up the steps then gently lowered his father down again. As he went to straighten, the sheikh lifted a pale bony hand to his youngest son's face and murmured something to him which sent Rafiq to his knees beside the divan and sent his covered head down.

The strong and the weak. It was a painful image that held everyone in its thrall because in those few seconds it was impossible to tell which man held the strength and which one was weaker.

'Hassan, go to him,' Leona said huskily. 'Rafiq needs you.'

But Hassan shook his head. 'He will not thank me,' he replied. And he was right; Leona knew that.

Instead Hassan turned his attention to causing yet another diversion by snapping his fingers to pull a small army of servants into use.

They came bearing trays of delicately made sweets and Arabian coffee and *bukhoor* burners, which filled the air with the smell of incense. The mood shifted, took on the characteristics of a traditional *majlis*, and the next time Leona looked the dais was surrounded by the old sheikhs from the desert tribes sitting around on the provided cushions while Sheikh Khalifa reclined on his divan enjoying their company.

Hassan took her father and Ethan with him and circulated the room, introducing them to their fellow guests. The timid Medina Al-Mahmud attached herself to Leona's side like a rather wary limpit and, taking pity on her, Leona found herself taking the older woman with her as they moved from group to group.

It was a success. The evening was really looking as if it was going to be a real success. And then from somewhere behind her she heard Sheikh Abdul say, 'A clever ploy. I am impressed by his strategy. For how many men here would now suspect Mr Hayes as his lovely wife's lover?'

She pretended not to hear, smiled her bright smile and just kept on talking. But the damage was done. The evening was ruined for her. For it had not once occurred to her that her father and Ethan were here for any other purpose than because Hassan wanted to please her.

Evie appeared at her side to save her life. 'Show me where I can freshen up,' she requested.

As Leona excused herself from those she was standing with, a hand suddenly gripped her sleeve. 'You heard; I saw your face. But you must not listen,' Medina advised earnestly. 'For he has the bad mouth and his wife is in purdah after Sheikh Hassan's visit yesterday.'

Sheikh Hassan's visit? Curiouser and curiouser, Leona thought grimly as she took a moment to reassure Medina before moving away with Evie Al-Kadah.

'What was that all about?' Evie quizzed.

'Nothing.' Leona dismissed the little incident.

But from across the room Hassan saw the green glint hit her eyes and wondered what had caused it. Had Evie let the proverbial cat out of the bag, or was it the timid Medina who had dared to stick in the knife?

He supposed he would soon find out, he mused heavily, and redirected his attention to whoever it was speaking to him, hoping he had not missed anything important.

The evening moved on; the old sheikh grew tired. His two sons appeared by the side of his divan. He did not demur when Hassan gently suggested he bid goodnight to everyone. Once again Rafiq lifted him into his wheelchair with the same gentleness that would be offered a fragile child. His departure was achieved quietly through a side door, as the old Sheikh himself had arranged.

Leona was standing with her father and Ethan as this quiet departure took place. 'How long?' Victor asked her gravely.

'Not very long,' she answered, then chided herself because Sheikh Khalifa wished his thirtieth celebration to be an occasion remembered for its hospitality, not as his obituary.

It was very late by the time people began leaving. Even later before Leona felt she could dare to allow herself a sigh of relief at how relatively pain-free the whole evening had turned out to be.

Which suddenly reminded her of something she still had to do that might not be as pain free. Her heart began thudding as Hassan came to take her hand and walk her towards the stairs. She could feel his tension, knew that his mind had switched onto the same wavelength as her own. Hand in hand they trod the wide staircase to the floor above. The door to the private apartments closed behind them.

'Did Evie bring—'

'Yes,' she interrupted, and moved right away from him. Now the moment of truth had arrived Leona found she was absolutely terrified. 'I don't want to know,' she admitted.

'Then leave it for now,' Hassan answered simply.

She turned to look anxiously at him. 'But that's just being silly.'

'Yes,' he agreed. 'But tomorrow the answer will still be the same, and the next day and the next.'

Maybe it was a good thing that the telephone began to ring. Hassan moved away from her to go and answer it. Thirty seconds later he was sending her a rueful smile. 'My father is restless,' he explained. 'Over-excited and in need of talk. Will you mind if I go to him, or shall I get Rafiq to—?'

'No,' she said quickly. 'You go.' She really was a pathetic coward.

'You won't…do anything without me with you?' he murmured huskily.

She shook her head. 'Tomorrow,' she promised. 'W-when I am feeling less tired and able to cope with…' *The wrong answer*, were the words she couldn't say.

Coming back to her, Hassan gave her a kiss of understanding. 'Go to bed,' he advised, 'Try to sleep. I will come back just as soon as I can.'

He was striding towards the door when she remembered. 'Hassan… My father and Ethan were invited here for a specific purpose, weren't they?'

He paused at the door, sighed and turned to look at her. 'Damage limitation,' he confirmed. 'We may not like it. We may object to finding such a demeaning act necessary. But the problem was there, and had to be addressed. *Inshallah*.' He shrugged, turned and left.

CHAPTER TWELVE

INSHALLAH—as Allah wills. It was, she thought, the perfect throwaway answer to an uncomfortable subject. On a dissatisfied sigh she moved across the room to begin to prepare for bed.

Already tucked out of sight in the drawer of her bedside cabinet lay the offerings Evie had brought with her from Behran. Just glancing at the drawer was enough to make her shudder a little, because the pregnancy testing kit had too much power for her comfort. So she turned away to pull on her pyjamas, slid into bed and switched off the light without glancing at the cabinet again. Sleep came surprisingly quickly, but then it had been a long day.

When she woke up, perhaps an hour later, she thought for a few moments that Hassan must have come back and disturbed her when he'd got into the bed. But there was no warm body lying beside her. No sign of life in evidence through the half-open bathroom door.

Then she knew. She didn't know how she knew, but suddenly she was up and pulling on a robe, frantically trying the belt as she hurried for the door. It was as if every light in the palace was burning. Her heart dropped to her stomach as she began racing down the stairs.

It was the sheikh. Instinct, premonition, call it what you wanted; she just knew there was something badly wrong.

On bare feet she ran down the corridor and arrived at his door to find it open. She stepped inside, saw nothing untoward except that neither the sheikh nor Hassan was there. Then she heard a noise coming from the room beyond, and with a sickening thud her heart hit her stomach as she made her way across the room to that other door.

On the other side was a fully equipped hospital room that had been constructed for use in the event of emergencies like the one Leona found herself faced with now.

She could not see the old sheikh because the doctors and nurses were gathered around him. But she could see Hassan and Rafiq standing like two statues at the end of the bed. They were gripping the rail in front of them with a power to crush metal, and their faces were as white as the *gutrahs* that still covered their heads.

Anguish lurked in every corner, the wretched sound of the heart monitor pulsing out its frighteningly erratic story like a cold, ruthless taunt. It was dreadful, like viewing a scene from a horror movie. Someone held up a hypodermic needle, clear liquid sprayed into the air. The lights were bright and the room bare of everything but clinical-white efficiency.

No, she thought, no, they cannot do this to him. He needs his room, with his books and his divan and his favourite pile of cushions. He needed to be surrounded by love, his sons, gentle music, not that terrible beep that felt to her as if it was draining the very life out of him.

'Switch it off,' she said thickly, walking forward on legs that did not seem to belong to her. 'Switch if off!' she repeated. 'He doesn't want to hear that.'

'Leona…' Hassan spoke her name in a hoarse whisper.

She looked at him. He looked at her. Agony screamed in the space between them. 'Tell them to switch it off,' she pleaded with him.

His face caved in on a moment's loss of composure. Rafiq didn't even seem to know that she was there. 'Don't…' he said huskily.

He wanted her to accept it. Her throat became a ball of tears as she took those final few steps then looked, really looked down at the ghost-like figure lying so still in the bed.

No, she thought again, no, they can't do this to him. Not here, not now. Her hand reached out to catch hold of one of his, almost knocking the nurse who was trying to treat him.

He felt so cold he might have been dead already. The tears moved to her mouth and spilled over her trembling lips. 'Sheikh,' she sobbed out, 'you just can't do this!'

'Leona…'

The thin, frail fingers she held in her hand tried to move. Oh, dear God, she thought painfully. He knows what is happening to him! 'Switch that noise off—switch it off!'

The fingers tried their very best to move yet again. Panic erupted. Fear took charge of her mind. 'Don't you dare bail on us now, old man!' she told him forcefully.

'Leona!' Hassan warning voice came stronger this time. He was shocked. They were all shocked. She didn't care.

'Listen to me,' she urged, lifting that frighteningly cold hand up to her cheek. The fingers moved again. He was listening. He could hear her. She moved closer, pushing her way past the doctor—a nurse—someone. She leaned over the bed, taking that precious hand with her. Her hair streamed over the white pillows as she came as close to him as she could. 'Listen,' she repeated, 'I am going to have a baby, Sheikh. Your very first grandchild. Tell me that you understand!'

The fingers moved. She laughed, then sobbed and kissed those fingers. Hassan came to grasp her shoulder. 'What do you think you are doing?' he rasped.

He was furious. She couldn't speak, couldn't answer, because she didn't *know* what she was doing. It had all just come out as if it was meant to. *Inshallah*, she thought.

'He can hear.' She found her voice. 'He knows what I am telling him.' Tremulously she offered Hassan his father's hand. 'Talk to him,' she pleaded. 'Tell him about our baby.' Tears were running down her cheeks and Hassan had never looked so angry. 'Tell him. He needs to hear it from you. Tell him, Hassan, please…'

That was the point when the monitor suddenly went haywire. Medics lunged at the sheikh, Hassan dropped his father's hand so he could grab hold of Leona and forcibly drag her aside. As the medical team went down in a huddle

Hassan was no longer just white, he was a colour that had never been given a name. 'You had better be telling him the truth or I will never forgive you for doing this,' he sliced at her.

Leona looked at the monitor, listened to its wild, palpitating sound. She looked at Rafiq, at what felt like a wall of horrified and disbelieving faces, and on a choked sob she broke free from Hassan and ran from the room.

Back down the corridor, up the stairs, barely aware that she was passing by lines of waiting, anxious servants. Gaining entrance to their apartments, she sped across the floor to the bedside cabinet. Snatching up Evie's testing kit, trembling and shaking, she dropped the packet twice in her attempt to remove the Cellophane wrapping to get the packet inside. She was sobbing by the time she had reached the contents. Then she unfolded the instruction leaflet and tried to read through a bank of hot tears, what it was she was supposed to do.

She was right; she was sure she was right. Nothing—nothing in her whole life had ever felt as right as this! Five minutes later she was racing downstairs again, running down the corridor in between the two lines of anxious faces, through doors and into the sheikh's room and over to her husband.

'See!' she said. 'See!' There were tears and triumph and sheer, shrill agony in her voice as she held out the narrow bit of plastic towards Hassan. 'Now tell him! *Please…!*' she begged him.

'Leona…' Hassan murmured very gently.

Then she heard it. The silence. The dreadful, agonising, empty silence. She spun around to look at the monitor. The screen was blank.

The screen was blank. 'No,' she breathed shakily. 'No.' Then she sank in a deep faint to the ground.

Hassan could not believe that any of this was really happening. He looked blankly at his father, then at his wife, then at the sea of frozen faces, and for a moment he actually thought he was going to join Leona and sink into a faint.

'Look after my son's wife.' A frail voice woke everyone up from their surprise. 'I think she has earned some attention.'

Before Hassan could move a team of experts had gone down over Leona and he was left standing there staring down at the bit of white plastic she had placed in his hand.

She was pregnant. She had just told him that this red mark in the window meant that she was pregnant. In the bed a mere step away his father was no longer fading away before his eyes.

Leona had done it. She'd brought him back from the brink, had put herself through the trauma of facing the answer on this small contraption, and she'd done both without his support.

'Courage,' he murmured. He had always known she possessed courage. 'And where was I when she needed my courage?'

'Here,' a level voice said. 'Sit down.' It was Rafiq, offering him a chair to sit upon. The room was beginning to look like a war zone.

He declined the chair. Leave me with some semblance of dignity, he thought. 'Excuse me,' he said, and stepped through the kneeling shapes round Leona, and bent and picked her up in his arms. 'But, sir, we should check she is...'

'Leave him be,' the old sheikh instructed. 'He is all she needs and he knows it.'

He did not take her far, only to his father's divan, where he laid her down, then sat beside her. She looked pale and delicate, and just too lovely for him to think straight. So he did what she had done with his father and took hold of her hand, then told her, 'Don't you dare bail out on us now, you little tyrant, even if you believe we deserve it.'

'We?' she mumbled.

'Okay, me,' he conceded. 'My father is alive and well, by

the way. I thought it best to tell you this before you begin to recall exactly why you fainted.'

'He's all right?' Her gold-tipped lashes flickered upwards, revealing eyes the colour of a sleepy lagoon.

I feel very poetic, Hassan thought whimsically. 'Whether due to the drugs or your bullying, no one is entirely certain. But he opened his eyes and asked me what you were talking about just a second after you flew out of the room.'

'He's all right.' Relief shivered through her, sending her eyes closed again. Feeling the shiver, Hassan reached out to draw one of his father's rugs over her reclining frame.

'Where am I?' she asked after a moment.

'You are lying on my father's divan, ' he informed her. 'With me; in all but effect, at your feet.'

She opened her eyes again, looked directly at him, and sent those major parts that kept him functioning into a steep decline.

'What made you do it?'

She frowned at the question, but only for a short moment, then she sighed, tried to sit up but was still too dizzy and had to relax back again. 'I didn't want him to go,' she explained simply. 'Or, if he had to go, I wanted him to do it knowing that he was leaving everything as he always wanted to leave it.'

'So you lied.'

It was a truth she merely grimaced at.

'If he had survived this latest attack, and you had been wrong about what you told him, would that have been a fair way to tug a man back from his destiny?'

'I'm pregnant,' she announced. 'Don't upset me with lectures.'

He laughed. What else was he supposed to do? 'I apologise for shouting at you,' he said soberly.

She was playing with his fingers where they pleated firmly with hers. 'You were in trauma enough without having a demented woman throwing a fit of hysterics.'

'You were right, though. He did hear you.'

She nodded. 'I know.'

'Here…' He offered her the stick of white plastic. Taking it back, she stared at it for a long time without saying a single word.

'It doesn't seem so important now,' she murmured eventually.

'The proof or the baby?'

She shrugged then pouted. 'Both, I suppose.'

In other words the delight she should be experiencing had been robbed from the moment. On a sigh, he scooped her up in his arms again and stood up.

'Where are you taking me now?' she questioned.

'Bed,' he answered bluntly. 'Preferably naked, so that I can hold you and our child so close to me you will never, ever manage to prise yourself free.'

'But your father—'

'Has Rafiq,' he inserted. 'And you have me.'

With that he pushed open the door to the main corridor, then stopped dead when he saw the sea of anxious faces waiting for news.

'My father has recovered,' he announced. 'And my wife is pregnant.'

There, he thought as he watched every single one fall to their knees and give thanks to Allah, that has killed two birds with one single stone. Now the phones could start buzzing and the news would go out to all corners of the state. By the time they arose in the morning there would not be a person who did not know what had taken place here tonight.

'You could have given me a chance to break the news to my own father.' Leona showed that her own thoughts were as usual not far from his own.

'He knows—or suspects. For I told him when I asked him to come here tonight. That was while we were still sailing the Red Sea, by the way,' he added as he walked them through the two lines of kneeling bodies. 'Raschid alerted me at Evie's instigation. And I am telling you all of this because I wish to get all my guilty machinations out of the way before we hit the bed.'

'You mean that Evie knew you suspected when I called her up yesterday and she didn't drop a hint of it to me?'

'They are sneaky, those Al-Kadahs,' he confided as he trod the stairs. 'Where do you think I get it from?'

'And your arrogance?'

'Al-Qadim through and through,' he answered. 'Our child will have it too, I must warn you. Plenty of it, since you have your own kind of arrogance too.'

'Maybe that's why I love you.'

He stopped halfway up the stairs to slash her a wide, white rakish grin. 'And maybe,' he said lazily, 'that is why I love you.'

She smiled, lifted herself up to touch his mouth with her own. He continued on his way while they were still kissing—with an audience of fifty watching them from the floor below.

Why not let them look? Sheikh Hassan thought. This was his woman, his wife, the mother of his coming child. He would kiss her wherever and whenever. It was his right. *Inshallah.*

Modern Romance™
...seduction and
passion guaranteed

Tender Romance™
...love affairs that
last a lifetime

Sensual Romance™
...sassy, sexy and
seductive

Blaze
...sultry days and
steamy nights

Medical Romance™
...medical drama on
the pulse

Historical Romance™
...rich, vivid and
passionate

MILLS & BOON®

Winner at

2001 IDEA INTERNATIONAL
DESIGN
EFFECTIVENESS
AWARDS

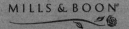

0702/73/MB38

Coming in July

The Ultimate Betty Neels Collection

* A stunning 12 book collection beautifully packaged for you to collect each month from bestselling author Betty Neels.

* Loved by millions of women around the world, this collection of heartwarming stories will be a joy to treasure forever.

2 FREE
books and a surprise gift!

We would like to take this opportunity to thank you for reading this Mills & Boon® book by offering you the chance to take TWO more specially selected titles from the Modern Romance™ series absolutely FREE! We're also making this offer to introduce you to the benefits of the Reader Service™—

- ★ FREE home delivery
- ★ FREE gifts and competitions
- ★ FREE monthly Newsletter
- ★ Exclusive Reader Service discount
- ★ Books available before they're in the shops

Accepting these FREE books and gift places you under no obligation to buy, you may cancel at any time, even after receiving your free shipment. Simply complete your details below and return the entire page to the address below. *You don't even need a stamp!*

YES! Please send me 2 free Modern Romance books and a surprise gift. I understand that unless you hear from me, I will receive 4 superb new titles every month for just £2.55 each, postage and packing free. I am under no obligation to purchase any books and may cancel my subscription at any time. The free books and gift will be mine to keep in any case.

P2ZEA

Ms/Mrs/Miss/Mr ....Initials.....................................
                                                       BLOCK CAPITALS PLEASE
Surname ....
Address ....

....
....Postcode.................................

Send this whole page to:
UK: FREEPOST CN81, Croydon, CR9 3WZ
EIRE: PO Box 4546, Kilcock, County Kildare (stamp required)